The Movie About Pusan

by

Larry Farmer

The Movie About Pusan

Cover Art by *The Wild Rose Press, Inc.*

The Wild Rose Press, Inc.
PO Box 708
Adams Basin, NY 14410-0708
Visit us at www.thewildrosepress.com

Publishing History
First Edition, 2022
Trade Paperback ISBN 978-1-5092-4060-9
Digital ISBN 978-1-5092-4061-6

Published in the United States of America

"Wilson," Sandra broke in. "I get that your uncles were here and it's more personal, but no one comes half way around the world to write their thesis. So I'm still waiting to hear more about why you chose to come here."

"You came here to write your thesis, Sandra," I countered.

"You know the answer to that. I wouldn't be here if my parents weren't here, and I'll be going back soon. How long are you staying? What all will you be doing?"

"There's a movie being made about the war. How we held on for dear life during the first year of the conflict. The theme of the movie is about dragging MacArthur to Korea to turn it around and how he did that. Turned it around and all."

"A movie?" Sandra quizzed. "They're making a movie about the Korean War? And that's why you came?"

"A movie about the last stand at Pusan and the victory at Inchon that turned the tide."

"What has that got to do with your thesis? I'm still not getting it."

"My thesis is about that period in the war, and since there's a movie being made, I wanted to be an extra in it and get a feel of it all. So, even more than personal, it's personal and adventurous. It will make the research and writing more fun."

"Seriously, Wilson?" Sandra gasped. "You are going to be an extra in a movie and write about it?"

"Not exactly, Sandra. I'll have to research just like normal. But it will still be informative to be in the movie. I can filter through fact from Hollywood."

Dedication

for Lisa Dixon Williams

Chapter 1

I hated the flight to Tokyo. From Los Angeles it took over fourteen hours that included stops in Hawaii and Guam. This was followed by a layover and another hop to my destination, Seoul. I had already endured a four-hour flight from the Dallas-Fort Worth metroplex to get to L.A.

South Korea was a developing country in 1977. All the Far East seemed to be developing rapidly. Except for the Communist countries, of course. Japan was challenging America economically thirty years after we devastated them in World War II. The mid 1970s also saw Taiwan flaunting a prosperity Chairman Mao had to live in denial about, while Hong Kong stayed British because Chairman Mao needed the prosperity from that colony as it trickled over into mainland China. Even Mao had to be pragmatic somewhere.

South Korea proved to be the biggest capitalist propaganda story imaginable, in fact. The Korean peninsula suffered division when the Communists took over the North after World War II. Then came the devastation from the war resulting shortly after that takeover. But, following the war, the South quickly expanded its economic base. There was much optimism.

Also animosity.

South Koreans didn't like their paternalistic

government. That domineering rule survived only because things could get worse, as the Communist dictatorship in North Korea proved. The haunting distraction of totalitarian North Korea kept the South Korean population focused on its economic prosperity, which capitalism provided. So they tolerated Syngman Rhee, their bullying first President. America, in turn, provided the military security the South needed.

An interesting place for my adventure, for sure—if you call writing a Master's thesis on the Korean War an adventure. This was a mission for which I felt more than ready, one that included the glamour of Hollywood thrown into the mix, with the movie I prepared to participate in while there.

Even though I planned to stay in South Korea for up to a year if need be, I brought little clothing. A sweatshirt, a jacket, two knit collared shirts, jeans, a pair of dress pants, some underwear and socks, as well as three T-shirts. Besides the cowboy boots I wore, I brought along a pair of leather moccasins, flip-flops, and a pair of dress shoes. South Korea was still a poor country, so I figured I could buy cheaply if I needed anything else.

As little clothing as I had, I barely had room for the two books I brought along in my hippie-style backpack. Such backpacks were used by vagabonds back in the sixties for their life on the road. A shoulder-width backpack with a cloth or polyester compartment approximately the depth of a small suitcase, it often towered above one's head.

One of the books I brought wasn't even on Korea, but on China instead. I liked the way it read, and China was close by and involved in that war. The book was very academic, with several footnotes on every page. I wanted the book not so much for information but for its style on which to model my Master's thesis.

The first thing the customs officer did after I arrived was to look at my plane ticket to make sure I had a return ticket home.

"What your first name?" he asked sternly. "Ticket say Wilson. That is last name. What is your first name?"

"Wilson is my first name. It is often a last name, but sometimes, like with me, it is also a first name."

"You come from America," he said as he inspected my passport further. "How long you stay Korea?"

"A couple of months," I lied.

"Your visa is for three months," he mused.

"Three is more than two," I said impatiently. "I probably will leave before the visa expires, but I want to check out some universities, do some research. I'm writing a Master's thesis, so I may need three."

"Student," he mumbled with a snarl. "How much money you have?"

"Five hundred dollars."

"Show."

I opened my money belt and got out my American traveler's checks. He inspected them and looked back at me before handing them over again.

"That is two hundred dollars," he sneered.

"Two hundred twenty," I corrected arrogantly. "That's enough. I'm staying at a hostel."

"That is not enough for three months here," he lectured me.

"I'm staying two months. I told you that."

"Visa say three months. Where is more money?"

I pulled out a credit card from my wallet and showed him.

"What university study you here?" he asked pointedly.

"I know a prof at Seoul Normal University."

"Seoul has many universities. What university?"

"I told you already. Seoul Normal University."

"Which university?"

"Seoul Normal University," I repeated, showing my frustration. "I don't know what you call it here. I'm American. That's what we call it. I'll find it. I know a professor here and will be staying with him."

"What is professor name?"

"Kim," I bluffed. "Professor William Kim."

"No professor named William here. This is Korea. What is name of professor?"

"I know him as William. He worked with missionaries back in Texas. I know how to find him. He is with history here. I'll find him. No worries."

"He's with me," a girl's voice from behind me said.

I turned to see who was acting as my rescuer. A tall slim girl with a long brown ponytail was walking my way from the long line of impatient passengers. She exuded self-confidence. And sex appeal.

"My father," she explained to the customs officer after she arrived, "is in the US Air Force here, and I wanted a chaperone while I visited him."

She walked past me to hand the officer her plane ticket. She pointed to a word on it.

"I came from Dallas with him," she said matter-of-factly. "We are students and are working on a paper together. I have family in the United States Air Force here, like I said, and talked my friend into coming with me. It made my parents feel more secure about me also. You can see he is tall and with muscles. I felt good to have him with me. He even has brown hair and blue eyes like I do, so we look like family. We'll stay with my parents, do some research, and leave in a couple of months. That is, if you let us into your country."

"If you came together, why you at back of line now?"

"I had more hand baggage than he did and told him to go on without me."

"That not a good gentleman," the officer admonished while continuing to look at the girl.

He then looked at me skeptically, back at her, and waved us through.

A smile eased onto my face as I walked toward the baggage claim with the girl. That was fun, I decided.

"Thanks," I said to her as I held out my hand. "Maybe you heard me tell the customs officer, but my name is Wilson."

"I'm Sandra," she replied as she shook my hand. "I saw you in Dallas. At the metroplex airport, I mean. We were on the flight together and made the same connections to Seoul. I guess it makes sense, since we were both headed here. I noticed you on the plane to L.A. and almost spoke when we boarded the flight to Japan and then here. I really am visiting my parents. They're stationed at an Air Force base here in Seoul, like I told Customs just now. I only wish I had gotten to know you somewhere sooner on this incredibly long and dreadful flight. But here we are, so that's good enough. Why don't you stay with us? My parents would love to have someone from back home."

I nodded as my smile increased.

"This worked out great. Thanks for rescuing me. I wish you had spoken to me, for sure. I don't know how I didn't notice you. I had a lot on my mind. Anyway, I'd love to meet your parents. But I should get a room at a hostel. Those are cheap. Tell your parents you met me, and see what they say. Maybe we can meet on the base and see if they are game to have me. They'll want to see you alone first. Is that okay? Let me find a hostel so you know where I'm staying, and we'll rendezvous tomorrow or something."

She scoped me out.

"You're welcome to stay, Wilson. It really will be all right. But suit yourself. Yes, we can meet on base tomorrow, and I'll introduce you. I'll tell them about you and arrange. All the more I should have said something to you somewhere on those dreadful flights we just endured."

After retrieving my backpack and helping her with her luggage, we headed for what looked to be a lobby with several booths by an exit. These booths surely had information for people like me. A cheap place to stay. Some kind of hostel.

"Good afternoon," a smiling young lady said with a mild accent as I approached her booth.

I was captured by the girl's exotic Asian looks. She was short, and her skin was almost as white as mine, but her dark hair and slanted eyes gave allure. My first Korean damsel.

"Hello," I greeted. "I need a place to stay. A place for a backpacker with little money."

"I have one for you. A hostel. Many from America and Europe stay there." She glanced quickly at Sandra.

"Also you? Are you staying with this gentleman?"

Sandra shook her head no.

The woman at the booth handed me a business card with an address. Written in pencil on the back of it was the name of a bus company with a bus number.

"You can find this bus just out front," the woman said. She turned and pointed at the street in front of the exit we were near. "Just go through that door and outside, and soon you will see a sign with the bus number I gave you. Show the driver this card, and he will know where to let you off. Sit near him. It is cheap and friendly here. Good luck and welcome."

"Give me a card also," Sandra broke in.

The girl did so. Sandra read from it, then looked at me.

"Wilson, my dear. This hostel has a phone number, so I will call you. I will even meet you there tomorrow and bring you to my parents' house on base. My father is a colonel at the base. He's with the Thirty-Fifth Fighter-Interceptor Group there, a pilot—or, he was. He's still attached to them, though. My parents will love to have someone from back home."

She reached inside the money belt strapped around her waist.

"Here," she said as she handed me a card of her own. "This is my parents' phone number. They are expecting me. I'm taking the shuttle bus to the base from here. I will arrange for you to stay in Seoul with us. I will be here a couple of weeks before I go back to Canyon—you know, west of Dallas. That's where I go to school. I'll be going back for the fall semester. Let us show you around. What are you doing here, by the way?"

"You go to school in Canyon?" I asked showing surprise. "I never met anyone from West Texas State."

"You've heard of us," she replied, with some surprise. "I'm working on my Master's degree there. So, answer me. You know about me. What about you? What are you doing here?"

"Working on my thesis. So there. Ha. We're kindred spirits. I'm working on a Master's too, at Texas A&M. Yes, why didn't we get to know one another on the way here?"

"An Aggie," she said excitedly. "My dad is an Aggie. That's why he was a pilot. He was in the Corps there at A&M."

"Me too. I was in the Corps. I was in the Aggie band."

"Oh, my God," she shrieked. "That is so cool. I can't believe this. It is torture now that we didn't sit together on the way here. My father is going to kill me that you are in a hostel and I didn't drag you home with me."

"Tomorrow," I assured her. "I have your phone number and you have mine. We'll meet and talk. Wherever you choose. I'll even stay with you. You may regret you asked me. I may never leave now. Ha."

"Good, you are welcomed forever. An Aggie. An Aggie BQ even."

"If you are going to call me a band queer, you can forget it."

"I can call you a BQ anytime I want, and so can my dad. So there."

I impulsively wanted to hold her hand as she walked me to my bus. I even considered giving her a kiss on the cheek as I left her at the curb and boarded. I settled for one last handshake instead.

The bus driver spoke little English but knew the address on the card and nodded he would let me know where to get off. I glanced out at Sandra one last time as the bus door closed and we drove away. I saw her blow a kiss my way as I waved goodbye.

Seoul was immense, and I felt uncomfortable as we plowed on and on through what looked to be a crammed neighborhood of cheap housing. As excited as I was over Sandra, riding the bus through Seoul tugged me back down to earth.

Most places we ventured through I would call ghetto. Among the things I studied in college was how third world countries, and even developing countries like South Korea, had one, sometimes two, huge cities that might contain half or more of the entire country's population. The impoverished countryside was constantly migrating to these centers, just hoping to find any kind of work at all. This bleak condition more than depressed me as we drove along—it scared me. I could sense how desperate the people must feel. What one had to do just to survive!

What I hoped to find in the hostel where I headed was knowledge. Street-wise backpacker knowledge on how to do my own surviving. That was one reason I wanted to spend my first night in Korea on my own. But mostly, I needed to know how best to get to Pusan. Would I be taking a boat to Pusan, or a train, or a bus? What should I expect in South Korea in general? Were the locals amenable to Americans? Did they think we were all rich? Were we imperialist pigs to them, to be shunned or worse?

The hostel was a short walk from the bus stop

where I was let off. At least this part of my pathfinding was easy.

"Five dollar," a short, jovial Korean man told me as I asked about a room. "You stay with one person. Five dollar good price. How long you stay?"

"I want to get to Pusan," I answered him.

"Pusan? You want Pusan? You must take bus. Better is train. But train more expensive."

"How much more expensive?"

"Not so much expensive. Train is better. Train station nearby. You stay one night here, tomorrow you go Pusan by train."

I was glad I'd exchanged a few dollars into won, their currency, back in L.A. I watched the owner of the hostel count the money I handed him. A smile spread on his face.

"Come with me," he said as I lifted my backpack to my shoulder. "I have room now with bed. You have roommate. He is nice man. He tell you about train and where to get food for eating. You are good here. We take care of you."

We walked outside into a courtyard, then on to the other end of the complex.

"There is bed," the owner said as he pointed to the side of the room where I would stay. "And locker. Put your things in locker. I hope you have lock for backpack. But it very safe here. No stealing. And very clean."

He abruptly left.

I was tired from the trip but too wound up from my new circumstances to lie down and rest. I wasn't particularly hungry, after my small meal on the plane, but decided eating was something to do for now.

I still had my business card of the hostel, just in case I wandered off and forgot where I was as I walked the nearby streets. It was time to scope out my environment.

I came upon a wooden food cart in the street just in front of the hostel. The hard-boiled eggs looked interesting. They were brown from having been soaked in soy sauce. So my travel guide informed me anyway. I preferred a cheap restaurant so kept walking. By the next block I found a cafeteria with open food stalls.

I had no idea about Korean food. I assumed it was much like Chinese and Japanese. There was rice, vegetables, and different kinds of meats. I inspected them and chose the safest-looking items, similar to Asian foods I'd had in the past.

"Why you no try kimchee?" the lady behind the cart asked me.

"What is that?" I asked.

"Kimchee is specialty of Korea. Recipe is kimchee, but food type here is potato. Kimchee is recipe for many foods."

"Potatoes sound good," I said. "I'll take some."

The girl made two scoops from the potatoes and put them on a plate for me.

"What else?" she asked.

"Only that. If this is a Korean recipe, I want to sample it first before I try other things."

There was an open table in the center of the eating area where I sat down. I scooped a potato and put it into my mouth. My lips and tongue instantly puckered. I wanted to gag and spit it out. It was very bitter. I looked at the guy at the next table as he snickered.

"You seem in discomfort," a young man with long

black hair said in an American accent.

"It's horrible," I groaned. "Horrible! God!"

I forced myself to swallow it.

"Actually, kimchee is very good. Maybe it's the potato recipe of it. Give it another try with another food."

He walked over, took my small bowl of potatoes, and returned to his table, where he dumped part of a bowl of vegetables in to mix with them.

"Here," he said with confidence. "Try these mixed vegetables. They aren't as strong. You'll like it, I'm sure."

I stared at him distrustfully, then sampled a spoonful.

"Wow," I said with a smile. "It doesn't taste anything like the potatoes. I mean the flavor."

"Kimchee is fermented. I figured you would like it. I would hate for you to miss out on their national dish. You'll like most of the dishes."

I nodded appreciatively and got up to get my own dish of kimcheed vegetables.

It was a good day, I decided. Especially meeting Sandra earlier. I'd made it to a hostel, found the train station to Pusan, and sampled satisfactorily a Korean dish. I was ready for tomorrow.

Chapter 2

"Hello, Sandra," I said early the next morning on the hostel's telephone.

"No, this is Sandra's mother," the voice on the other end said. "Is this Wilson? Are you Sandra's friend from Aggieland that she met yesterday on the plane?"

"We met at customs in Seoul. She rescued me."

"She does that well," her mother said with a chuckle. "I cannot believe you chose to stay at a hostel when right here we are on base. And you're a BQ to boot. My husband was in Filthy Fifth. Y'all used to have water fights against each other in the Corps."

"Everyone had water fights with us in the Corps," I answered, warmed from the memories of my college undergrad days.

"Listen, we have your business card, I mean of your hostel. You stay right where you are. We have a car. Sandra and I will be there shortly to pick you up. Is that okay? We have so much to share."

"Yes, ma'am. I can't believe someone from back home. But I guess there are a lot of Aggies in Seoul attached to the military."

"That's the truth. Anyway, you stay where you are. We'll find you. It may be a while. We'll have to drive through part of the city. Seoul, you know. Read a book or something. Hang tight."

"I'll wait in front of the hostel entrance," I

explained. "I'm tall, and Sandra knows what I look like. Just stop at the curb there, and I'll hop in."

It seemed I was waiting outside forever before Sandra's mother appeared, even though I read for quite a while first, in the hostel.

Sandra and her mother looked very much alike, I decided after I hopped into the car when they arrived. Especially with the short, wavy hair.

"Is that all of your belongings?" Sandra's mother asked as we rode along. "I mean, everything? You didn't leave anything behind in the hostel where you stayed?"

"It's everything. I travel light."

"You'll feel easily at home here after hassling with your flight and your hostel. You'll enjoy the base, I think. A bit stiff and overregulated, but a feeling of home to it."

The warmth of Sandra's mother eased any feeling of homesickness I had.

"There's the gym to our left now, Wilson," her mother said soon after we entered the military base. "If you ever want to work out. It's not far from our house."

It was a small two-bedroom wooden cottage where they lived. Simple but adequate housing for a family overseas.

"My husband is in Okinawa," Sandra's mother informed as she guided me to the couch in the living room. "Y'all can talk about your college days when he returns. He'll like that. Would you like some coffee while we chat?"

"Sure," I said.

"I can get it, Mom," Sandra offered.

"So, Wilson, what brings you here? You never

said."

"Forget coffee," Sandra said as she sat back down. "I want to hear this. We never talked about why we're here. I guess I did. But why are you here, Wilson? You mentioned your thesis for your Master's. But why here?"

"I had two uncles who fought in the war here," I replied. "It made things more personal to me to be here. I think I will enjoy the research more with that personal background."

"That makes sense," Sandra's mother commented. "Yes, it will help your focus. Even a labor of love, in a way."

"The Far East is so exotic to me anyway," I commented further. "So. Do you like it here?"

"Well, it's certainly interesting. We've been to Okinawa, to Germany, and Italy. Now here. They move you around a bit in the military. You never feel quite at home before you must leave again. We'll be ready to retire soon. I mean, we are retired from the military already, but after a few years in the civil service we can go back to Texas and stay put. I like it here, knowing we have that to look forward to."

"Wilson," Sandra broke in. "I get that your uncles were here and it's more personal, but no one comes half way around the world to write their thesis. So I'm still waiting to hear more about why you chose to come here."

"You came here to write your thesis, Sandra," I countered.

"You know the answer to that. I wouldn't be here if my parents weren't here, and I'll be going back soon. How long are you staying? What all will you be doing?"

"There's a movie being made about the war. How we held on for dear life during the first year of the conflict. The theme of the movie is about dragging MacArthur to Korea to turn it around and how he did that. Turned it around and all."

"A movie?" Sandra quizzed. "They're making a movie about the Korean War? And that's why you came?"

"A movie about the last stand at Pusan and the victory at Inchon that turned the tide."

"What has that got to do with your thesis? I'm still not getting it."

"My thesis is about that period in the war, and since there's a movie being made, I wanted to be an extra in it and get a feel of it all. So, even more than personal, it's personal and adventurous. It will make the research and writing more fun."

"Seriously, Wilson?" Sandra gasped. "You are going to be an extra in a movie and write about it?"

"Not exactly, Sandra. I'll have to research just like normal. But it will still be informative to be in the movie. While I do my research on the war and all, I can filter through fact from Hollywood. It will be fun."

Sandra looked at her mother.

"Wow, Mom. Wow. Yeah. Hey, I want to do that."

"Sandra, dear…" Her mother sighed, her concern obvious. "You're only here a couple of weeks before you have to get back to finish so you can graduate next year."

Sandra shook her head while looking past her mother.

"No, Mother. I'm going to call my committee

chairman. I'll put my thesis on hold. I'm going with Wilson."

"Sandra, you are ready to graduate. What am I going to tell your father?"

"You're going to get me in trouble, Sandra," I said with a whine. "I didn't come here to make waves."

"This has nothing to do with you, Wilson," Sandra returned defiantly. "This has to do with the fact that I want to do what you're doing. My chairman will understand. It's okay. What's a semester on hold? No big deal."

"Your chairman might understand," her mother said, "but I'm not sure your father will."

"Sandra, damn it," I whined further. "Your parents are going to be bugged they ever met me. Give me a break."

"That's okay, Wilson," Sandra's mother consoled. "Sandra is always full of surprises."

"And this is why, Mom. Life is fun. Serious, but fun. I'll get it all done."

"Listen, Sandra," I broke back in. "I better go. I don't want any part of ruining your life."

"How is this going to ruin my life, Wilson? What's so special about you that you get to do all of this and I have to just go by the book? I'm going to be an extra. Where do I go? What do I do? What are you going to do in the movie?"

"I don't know yet," I answered with a grimace. "I'm just going to take a train in the morning and find where they are filming and see. That's all I know."

"I'm going with you."

"Sandra, I'm leaving in the morning. You need to talk to your chairman and your dad."

"If I have to find you, Wilson, I'm going to kill you. You better call me when you get there and let me know how it's going and where to meet you. I'll take care of my dad and my chairman."

I was pleased with the thought of seeing Sandra again. If we got that far.

"Okay, it's a go," I said with a glint in my eye. "I've got your phone number. You take care of things about you, and I'll blaze a path for us. Sounds good."

Sandra had a glint in her eyes to match my own. It made me wish her mother wasn't around.

Chapter 3

The train ride to Pusan was long but enjoyable. I held onto my backpack as we rode, clutching it on my lap even though the seat next to me was empty. I wasn't worried about it getting stolen as much as that I could run off without it from some stupor.

I liked trains, and the countryside was green and rolling as I looked out the window. People working the fields appeared as though they were living out a painting. At each stop were vendors selling food at the side of the train. Most of these vendors were on short platforms in small towns or villages. I had the milk run, it seemed. Hello, Korea.

Pusan seemed another vast and endless ghetto when I arrived. I couldn't tell the difference between it and what I had seen of Seoul, though Seoul was bigger. Both were too big for me. Soon after arrival, I found the bus for the part of town where there were hostels for people like me. Hopefully someone in the hostel would know about the movie I aspired to be in.

"Here," the bus driver said to me. "You go here. Many Americans in hostel. Backpack Americans here. You get off now."

I looked to my left, then my right, before stepping off onto the curb. I hated this part of travelling. The not knowing what I'm doing part.

"To left," the driver instructed, to hurry me along.

I walked the sidewalk, hoping to see any clue of a hostel. A few feet in front of me was an old two-story stone building with a sign in Korean script, but also in English.

Busan English Hostel, a sign on it read. Busan was how Pusan was spelled, but with the B pronounced P. Either way, this must be the place to be, I decided. This was pretty straightforward, beckoning the likes of me.

"Hello," a smiling middle-aged man said from behind a counter just inside.

"You have a room?" I asked cautiously.

"Yes. Many American and English here. Many European here. All speaking English here."

I nodded and let out a smile of my own. This was the place. And the price was right, too. Five dollars per day. If I got hired as an extra, it left me plenty to live on. If not, it gave me time to interview people for my thesis.

Besides the stone building by the street, there were six wooden buildings behind it on the hostel grounds, each one slightly bigger than the size of a middle-class bedroom back home. Each building was divided into two separate rooms for the paying customers. One of the wooden buildings was for the owner, but also had two shower rooms attached to it with toilets in each. A shower room for men and one for women.

. These wooden buildings faced each other three to a side, with an inner area of tables where the guests could mingle. In the center of these tables was one more wooden booth, with a desk and a television set underneath its roof.

Inside the room where I was assigned were two cots for beds that folded. One of the cots had a long sponge-type mattress on it. Apparently, I had a roommate. To the side of the door was a chest of drawers. There was a steel bar on the window sill on the opposite end of the room, with a backpack locked to it.

After securing my gear, I went out to the sidewalk in front of the hostel complex. Nearby was a food vendor. It was time to try out the cuisine. I scoped out both the raw vegetables, such as onions and tomatoes, and the cooked vegetables. There were also trays with different kinds of sauces, as well as bins of rice.

"Chicken," I told a woman as I pointed to a drumstick from the selection of meats.

"Very good," she said with a smile. "Choose, please."

I pointed again at a drumstick.

"Very good," she repeated.

I then pointed at the rice. I hesitated to get vegetables in case there was a surprise waiting for me such as the kimcheed potatoes back in Seoul.

"Onion sauce," the lady informed me as I looked at a bowl of dark brown sauce.

It looked like soy sauce except it had some powdered spices in it. I then checked the dark brown sauce in the bowl next to it.

"Soy sauce," she explained.

I knew I liked soy sauce, but decided to try the onion sauce.

She poured a ladle on top of the rice and handed me the paper plate where she had placed the food. I smiled my approval and handed her a wad of bills from my money belt. She grabbed a few that totaled less than a dollar in equivalent. I smiled yet again.

I took my food back to my room, then mumbled in

21

frustration when I saw I'd forgotten to bring any plastic utensils.

"I'll go native." I dug into my meal with my fingers.

The food was beyond good, especially with the onion sauce. Onion sauce. I had to remember that. Better than soy sauce was onion sauce. Or this version of it, anyway.

Finally, some sleep. But not for long. With barely an hour on my cot, the wooden door to my room burst open. I stared. A medium height, slim young man with short curly black hair walked toward his cot, plopped down, and stared back at me.

"I woke you up," he said in an accent I couldn't place.

"That's okay," I assured.

He walked over to me and stooped while extending his hand to shake mine.

"Chaim," he said.

"What?" I asked.

"Chaim," he repeated. "Spelled like chain but with an m instead of an n for the last letter. Americans call me Chaim, pronounced like chain, in fact, if they read my name before I can introduce myself. It is pronounced like a k at the beginning, khime, like chime, but pronounced with a kuh sound instead of chuh. You'll figure it out. I am Israeli. Chaim is an Israeli name."

I mused on all he'd just said before extending my hand to shake his.

"I'm Wilson," I said. "Like Woodrow Wilson. I'm not named after him. After some guy my dad knew in World War II, I was told. Anyway, good to meet you,

Chaim. Looks like we're roommates."

"What brings you here?" he asked.

"There's a movie about the Korean War that I want to be an extra in."

His eyes opened widely.

"You are in luck, my friend. I am an extra in that very movie. This movie you talk about is about the Pusan Perimeter, perhaps? That's the only movie I know of going on. At least Hollywood movie. Matt Jillette is the director. Three thousand extras like me. We get thirty-five dollars a day for this. Mostly standing around. But it is fun."

"Yes. That's the one. I came from Texas to be in it."

"You're in it?" Chaim asked amazed.

I shook my head no.

"I came here to write my college thesis and will use this movie as a platform for that."

"You came all the way from Texas to be an extra in a movie," he said in disbelief.

"Why are you here?"

"I just finished my basic training in the Israeli Army and wanted to get away for a while. Just travel, I mean. I bought a ticket to India, then got a ticket for just a few hundred dollars that takes you all the way to Tokyo by way of Bangkok, Hong Kong, Taipei, Seoul, then Tokyo. I have a year to use it. Then I will fly back to Tel Aviv. I'm actually from Haifa. When I got here, all the Europeans and Americans were telling me about this movie and thirty-five dollars a day to be an extra. So, why not? That's a lot of money."

"And they still need extras?"

He nodded yes. "Just go with me tomorrow. We'll

23

take a bus. They meet at a US Air Force base. Most of the extras are US soldiers and airmen. No one will know you just got here and wouldn't care anyway. There are so many from Europe and America here already, besides the soldiers. You will have many friends. Good memories."

I couldn't believe my luck. So easy.

"How long have you been here, Chaim?"

"A month."

"The whole time with the movie?"

"Yes."

"So how long has the movie been going on?"

"Two months."

"Two months? I just read about it a couple of weeks ago."

"Don't worry. You have plenty of time to be in this movie, from what I've heard. I'm not sure, actually. You'll get to meet the movie stars, or at least hang around them sometimes. Judy Mangum is the leading starlet. Roy Holland plays a Marine. Lance Talbert plays MacArthur. He's seventy years old, but with makeup he looks just like MacArthur."

"Lance Talbert is Shakespearean. British."

"He's an actor and a big name. Speaks with a good American accent for the movie. That's what actors do. Especially for two million dollars."

"Wow. He gets two million dollars?"

"And he's not ashamed to say that's why he took the job. Puts a major name to the actors, not that the others aren't stars. But he gives things a classy touch just having a name as big as his. So, two million dollars was worth it to the producers."

"My God. I'm going to faint if I meet any of these

guys."

"I haven't gotten to meet anyone yet, but at least I see them every day. Sometimes even close up. Sometimes we're just a few feet away. It's hard not to drool. Especially around Judy Mangum. She is beautiful."

"Oh, man." I swooned. "I hope I don't meet any of them. I will drool. Literally."

"Stick with me until you find your way. Making a movie is boring. Nothing exciting about any of it, except being around movie stars. And the novelty of it makes it fun."

I tried to picture the setting he described. I was awestruck just thinking about it.

"Just stick with me," Chaim repeated.

Chapter 4

The US government was cooperating with the making of this movie since it presented the military in a good light. The movie was good for morale and good for recruiting. And with the use of three thousand extras, most of them GIs, it helped pad the incomes of the troops.

Part of the cooperation included access to US Air Force facilities in and around Pusan for the film crew, including extras. That was convenient for everyone—in particular, the likes of me. I now had outlets to good old American food. Nothing against Korean food, but now my favorite foods were available in my life again. Things like hamburgers and tacos. Access to the base also got me into the gym for a good workout. I missed lifting weights, and now I had all the equipment I needed at my disposal. I even preferred jogging on base on their track.

But there was a negative. A big one.

I was from rural Texas and a descendant of war heroes. I was patriotic and admired the military. Many students from college campuses in my generation shunned the military, even ridiculed it. I tried to be open minded about these mockers of our military men, reminding myself that freedom of speech was one of the things the military was duty bound to protect. Now, however, I saw GIs all around me and was not impressed with what I saw. In fact, I was disgusted. I didn't want to be. But the more I saw of the military, the more the disgust came out. It was one thing to decide they weren't baby killers and goons, but another stereotype about GIs was that they couldn't do anything besides the military. Meaning not just goons but incompetent goons. But here they were, staring me in the face. Very few GIs I saw had much personality. And it seemed like anyone physically fit was weeded out. Short, ugly, and with a pot gut was the norm.

What did my Israeli friend think of them? I was afraid to find out.

"Before we finish basic training in Israel," Chaim informed me after we came in from my first day on the set, "we have to stay awake for three straight days."

I knew military-related training had to be hard in Israel, just from knowing the constant survival environment they lived in. Still, I listened with awe at the stories he related to me.

"And during those three days, we had to run six, even nine miles at a time."

"Real miles or do you mean kilometers?" I asked.

"We use the metric system," he explained, "but since we were part of the British mandate before independence, we know miles and pounds also. We interchange easily. I am talking miles."

"I was an athlete back home in Texas," I commented, "and grew up on a farm. I know hardship. But y'all go beyond."

"Everyone hates the army back home," he said. "But I don't mean like we heard about Americans during Vietnam. We have the luxury to hate it. We have to be in it, and we believe we should be in it. Israel has to do more than adequately survive. We have to be so powerful the enemy feels intimidated. They may still want to annihilate us, but we have to make them feel it is futile, just to limit how much they try."

"They try hard enough," I responded.

"Exactly. And it will never end. But intimidation is a weapon, nevertheless. Just one of many. So even twenty-mile runs at times are part of our training. But as we ran during the three days of no sleep, we were so tired that some would fall asleep during the run."

I tried to picture falling asleep during a run. I could understand crapping out, or even collapsing, but to just fall asleep while jogging, I couldn't fathom it.

"Hating the army keeps us going," Chaim explained further. "You need to remember why you have to be in the army to keep from really hating it, but you have to allow yourself to hate it some just to keep you going. No one wants to be here doing this. But we must. We are always shorthanded. We have so few troops, compared to the enemy, that we have to do so much more than just be equal to them. We must defeat and devastate them—just to survive, you might say. We have better equipment and weapons, but we have to be better trained and better tempered also, more determined to survive than they are to wipe us out. Hate for the sake of hate, or as a boost to war, is not enough. Hate is even an Arab downfall. That is their most powerful weapon, hate, but it really limits them more than to be an asset. Hate just for hate is self-demeaning. Self-destructive. I can tell you, the Israelis' biggest weapon is not our training or our weapons, it is love. Love for heritage, for history, for our country and fellow Israelis. Jews are the world's outcasts wherever we go, throughout any period in history. So we have to be Jews. Proud Jews. Not boastful, but armed with ethics and purpose."

I nodded my head in agreement, even though it was dark in the room, so he couldn't see.

"I was ashamed today," I told him, "when I saw the state of our armed forces. I remember the Vietnam era and how everyone hated the military. I didn't hate it. I wasn't in it, but so many in my generation did hate it back then. Whether you were in it or not, everyone my age seemed to hate it. I suppose the condition our military is in now is from all that. Morale was more than down during Vietnam, and there was so much negativity attached to the military. I'm so ashamed for someone like you to see this."

"It scared me when I first saw these soldiers," Chaim said in a reserved, analyzing tone.

"Why did it scare you?"

"Maybe there is a better word than scared," he mused. "The whole world depends in so many ways upon America. There is the Soviet Union, there is China, there are the Arab countries. America has military and economic might to thwart these threats to the Western democracies. American power also buys cooperation from any hoped-for ally. Israel is a regional power. Some say a world power, but even where that may be true, we are so small. America is big. So I know America has great weapons and great alliances with NATO, but if your people are not up to the task, no matter how many bombs and dollars you have, you are vulnerable. I see these soldiers, and the ones here on this base and others around are not the elite of your military. Thank goodness you also have very powerful and competent elite forces.

"But so much also depends on your common soldier. Your common soldier is not up to task. Even the elite forces must come from the masses. How many Americans even bother to join the military? In Israel we all get drafted. All the more reason to hate our duty, a duty we believe in and want to uphold, but it gives us the luxury to complain. But the Americans that volunteer willingly to be in your military, from those that do, if you take away the elite soldiers from this group of common soldiers, these common soldiers provide so little for the military. It frightens me for Israel and Europe, but also for everywhere else that needs stability in the world. For America itself. There is more than controversy about the Vietnam war that is the cause of this."

"I agree with you," I said with a sigh. "I was hoping I was wrong in feeling that way, but you said exactly how I feel. There is a naïveté with my generation that scares me badly. Much of my generation seems to think the only naïve ones are the ones who join the military. That's what the hip crowd chirps anyway. Well, they see a naïveté that does indeed exist with our soldiers, but the critics of our military are even more naïve."

"We had a boring day today at the base, didn't we?" Chaim asked, off on his own thoughts. "We never even got off the base. You and I had to stand around the whole time. They were setting up for a big scene tomorrow, so we were left to ourselves. But keep hanging around with me, Wilson. On the set, I mean. It is bad enough we have these out-of-shape soldiers without much brain power to defend your country. To defend the whole free world, in fact. However, Matt Jillette is not going to use these dull soldiers for special scenes. You are big and athletic. We must make ourselves ready to be chosen. We must be obvious to the directors and staff on the movie set. When they prepare for special scenes, we must stand out. So, be in a position to be obvious. To be discovered, as they say. I always hear how some movie star was discovered at some obscure setting. That is us. Be ready to be discovered. Let Matt Jillette seek us out and find us."

To hear Chaim speak excited me. I never pictured being in a movie. But here I was. Today was indeed boring, but I was still in a movie. Even though I wasn't used on my first day, I still got my thirty-five dollars. I was now a movie actor. Sort of. Boring or not, it pumped me up to think about it.

I thought of Sandra back in Seoul. I did not want to lure her here for nothing, but surely she had a place in all of this. Something to make for herself in this situation.

"In these GI scenes with the extras," I threw out to Chaim, "is there a place for women?"

"There were women with us today."

"I saw a couple, but I wasn't sure what they did."

"They weren't used today either. There are girls here at this complex where we are now. You saw some with us on the bus, and they went with us to the set and back again. When we came back to the hostel, you left to go eat on your own, but the rest of us went out together. We know each other now. Chums, as you say. There are over ten of us here at this hostel involved in this movie, from all over America and Europe. Four of them are girls. They are used in scenes now and then and get their thirty-five dollars just like the rest of us."

"I didn't know who was who or what anyone did. You and I separated as soon as we got on base. And hardly anyone was used today. You knew what you were doing. No one else seemed to. I didn't know what was going on."

"All of us at this complex, except for the Koreans, are extras in the movie. You will get to know them easily."

"I have a friend from Texas. She's visiting her parents in Seoul. They are attached to the military. This girl and I met on the plane. You make it sound like there's a place for her."

"Yes, yes. She will easily fit in. It's one large but friendly mob. Call her. Tell her there is a place for her if she is interested."

I was smiling widely enough I was sure Chaim could see it even in the dark.

Chapter 5

"I have some good news for you, Sandra," I said excitedly on the hostel telephone.

"Hey, what's up, there, Wilson? Where are you calling from?"

"Pusan. It's a go here with this movie. I'm an extra in it, like I hoped. Just thought I'd let you know. It's fun. Well, I was bored my first day. They ended up not using us. At least the group I was with. But today was my first real day—I got to get killed in a scene. They picked me randomly and told me and some others that when we heard an explosion to pretend to feel the blast and fall down dead."

"Wow, maybe you'll win an Oscar for this. Great. Ha."

"Actually, I'm not happy with my performance. I died okay, I think. That was easy enough, but when I was laying on the ground I started evaluating if I died realistically. Was I believable? And while thinking it over, I started shaking my head, picturing how I could have done better. I didn't shake my head much, but I'm sure it was on film and they might edit me out. That part of the scene, I mean. I don't know."

"Look at this guy," she swooned. "Boy, you are a natural somehow. You take this stuff seriously. Go for it, Wilson."

"Anyway, about you. Come on over here. There's

an Air Force base in Pusan, and that's where we meet every morning. At the EM club—you know, the enlisted men's club. The guards at the entrance will know where to tell you to go. Come and find us. I'm staying with an Israeli guy at a hostel in town. There's about a dozen of us staying here. Most from America, but there is a guy from England, a girl from Sweden, and a guy from Nepal. I never met anyone from Nepal before. A bunch of Korean girls from around hang out at the hostel with us but don't live there. They're local college students and like to mix with us at night after we get back from the set."

"What are all these Americans and such doing there? Did they come just for the movie like you did?"

"I'm the only one that did that. The rest are all travelers. Here by way of Hong Kong, or on the way to Japan or something. But the movie is going on, and some people hear about it, and a few of them hop on the Hollywood train, so to speak. It's fun. They are fun. Interesting. You'll make it more interesting."

"Are there any girls? Besides the Swedish one. I might get too much attention."

"There are four girls. Two Americans, a Dutch girl, and the Swede. Everyone is in their twenties. Male and female. All in their twenties."

"Okay. I'm on my way. I'll find this Air Force base. It's the one inside Pusan?"

"On the edge, yes. Just get to Pusan and find the one Air Force base inside or on the edge of the city. Listen, Sandra, if you get here during the day and we're off somewhere, just find where we gather on base when we get back and wait for us at that EM club I mentioned. I'll show you the hostel after we meet at the base. Call me if the worst happens. Here's my number…" I gave her the number of the Pusan hostel where I was staying and had her repeat it to me. "I'll be looking for you. I'm assuming you got things squared away with your committee chairman and parents."

"Yes. My chairman wasn't too happy about it at first, but the idea grew on him. I needed your help with that, though."

"How can I help? Do I need to call him? Why would he care about me?"

"Because we're engaged to be married." She giggled. "Wilson? Hey, Wilson! Earth speaking. Hey!"

"We're engaged to be married?" I asked with an exaggerated moan. "Thanks for telling me. That is something I should know, for sure."

"Well, when I heard him concerned about my maturity level, putting my thesis on hold and all to be an extra in a movie perhaps, I figured I better hit him with more serious stuff. Even a college professor can understand about getting married. So."

"Great, Sandra. Great. Yeah, great you bothered to tell me. Anyway, head on out. We don't have to sleep together just because we're engaged. We can be old-fashioned. I'll just stay with the Israeli I share a room with at the hostel."

"My parents will be thrilled to hear you won't take advantage of me."

She was going to do this. Be in the movie with me. Stay at the same hostel as me. Thinking about it warmed me up. I began to wonder why it did.

With all the free time we had on the set the next day, I kept thinking of her. I couldn't get her off my mind, in fact. I was nervous in anticipation as I entered the EM club when our van arrived from the set. Then there she was, sitting at a table near the door, reading a book as I entered.

"Sandra," I called out.

She turned toward me and broke into a smile.

"Wilson, yay, you're here! Just like you said. I found the place and sure enough, *voilà*, here you are."

She got up and walked toward me. Without hesitation she gave me a hug, even placing her head on my chest affectionately.

"So good to see you, guy," she said, looking up at me.

"You too, Sandra. I love you're here. I found you a room at the hostel. With the Swedish girl I mentioned."

I turned to the group of extras who had arrived from the set with me.

"These are your new companions," I said to Sandra while looking at them. "The blonde sexy one there in the middle of this rabble is Sunshine, your new roommate, this Swede I mentioned. No need to introduce everyone now. They know who you are, and we'll get chummy on the ride to the hostel."

It charmed me to see how easily Sandra fit in with the others. And once she moved into her room, the two of us, Sandra and me, split off to my favorite restaurant.

"So, this is a marvelous onion sauce," I said as I poured it over my steamed rice. "Try the chicken. It's steamed chicken, rather bland, but not so bland when you pour the sauce over it."

"You should be on a travel show," she said with a chuckle. "My personal guide here."

"It's exciting to be half way around the world," I replied as an explanation. "I always loved history and geography and things like that. Now here I am, smack dab in all my fantasies. Living my own personal documentary. Meeting new people and cultures and trying the local cuisines. Nothing fancy so far. Just the exotic day to day."

"With a movie thrown in," she added with a wink.

I nodded while easing into a grin.

"Have you written much on your thesis?" she asked.

I let out a huff.

"Barely crosses my mind, to be honest. I'm so into being in Korea and making a movie and meeting people, you know. It's not just Koreans in my life that's new to me, but people at the hostel. And for sure Hollywood creatures on the set every day."

"Are you shaking off your thesis, then? You're scaring me here, Wilson. I have to write my thesis. I mean, I *have* to. Period. Plus, my parents trusted me and let me come here. I can't let them down. This isn't just about me."

"Yeah." I groaned. "I know. I know. I'll do it. Not now. It would be a distraction right now. I really will begin soon, though."

"I need to get some bearings too, I admit," she said in a concerned tone of voice. "But you've been here in Korea almost a week. I can't wait that long. I'll get out of focus."

"Focus. That's a word. Yeah, you're right. I'm going to have to get started. I need to focus."

I stared at her a moment, wanting to change the subject.

"You didn't get to see Lance Talbert today," I teased. "If you get to stay with me and my crowd of extras in the movie, you'll see him soon. Probably, anyway. He's in about half the scenes I'm involved in."

"That would be exciting, for sure. Maybe I can get a picture. Do you have a picture of him?"

"I'd feel cheap for that," I replied. "I don't know why. Like this fan club groupie. I have to say I nearly fainted when I first met him. I don't know why I would feel so cheap getting a picture."

"I have a small Instamatic," she said. "I'll have it in one of my blouse pockets. Or wear khaki with pouches and put it there. We'll get us a picture."

"You've got to stay with me somehow," I said in a deliberate tone. "It should be easy to accomplish that, I suppose, but somehow we've got to share all of this together. To be there for one another."

I loved the smile that broadened on her when I said that. She liked me. It was obvious. I was afraid to believe it too much, not trusting that it wouldn't go to my head. But she liked me, and I held on to that. The feelings were mutual. I could feel them inside. I was going to check this out.

Chapter 6

One of the assistant directors was from Greece. They called him Freddy. A short, skinny, annoying guy with a beard. I tried not to judge him. I could picture the pressure on him to prove himself. This might be his one shot at getting any kind of recognition. But he had little personality and didn't do much besides herd us around and shut us up. So, judge I did.

"Quiet on the set," Freddy barked through his megaphone. "Quiet, please. Quiet on the set."

We were already quiet. To keep three thousand people silent, we did indeed have to be reminded of our place. If he did something else behind the scenes, I didn't know. However, every encounter between scenes was this same line of shrieking from him. Occasionally he helped select extras to herd into another area for some other scene that needed a mob of soldiers.

There was a group of stuntmen that helped with the herding also. But in a more productive way. These were the ones Chaim alerted me about. The ones that picked certain extras for action scenes. Chaim was near me, and I keyed on his focus. How he followed their moves as they went from one group of extras to another. They were looking for fresh meat, I was sure.

"They are coming our way, Wilson," Chaim said just above a whisper. "They have something in mind. Stand straight. Look serious. Be casual and don't stare, but keep them in your sight. This may be our chance."

Impatiently, the stuntmen scoped out the soldiers around, but quickly left everyone behind.

"Here, Wilson," Chaim said pointedly. "Here comes the head stuntman. I've seen him before. He's looking directly at us. Don't look back at him, but keep him visible and look serious."

"You two are extras," the stuntman said matter-of-factly to Chaim, then to me. "Am I right? Waiting for another battle to fight in?"

"Yes," Chaim replied. "We just charged that hill behind us and were told to wait until an assistant director needed us."

"Forget that," he said.

"Yes, good," another of the stuntmen said while inspecting us. "You'll do. We have six extras now, with you two. That's all we need."

The one Chaim called the head stuntman now looked at me.

"Your hair is a bit too long. It's short enough for today's Army, but this is Korea in the early fifties, and we need you to be Marines. Marines have very short hair. Yours is bushy. We need you to get a haircut when we get back to the base this afternoon. Get a Marine haircut. There is theoretically a war going on, and you are out in the field, so we don't need a bootcamp Marine haircut. But definitely not bushy like it is. You're Marines, and we need you to look the part, so there is no guesswork for any of your scenes. An inch on top and white sidewalls around the edges. Is that understood?"

He turned to leave but then waved for us to follow him.

He used the word "scenes." Plural. And it seemed as if we were with them now. I felt the rush inside.

"Sandra," I yelled out hoping she could hear.

She was nearby, and I saw her look my way. I motioned my head for her to follow me. I wanted her as close by me as possible. Not just for moral support, but for any opportunity that might come her way in which I could encourage.

The stuntmen brought us to an open field. There was a tent nearby for the actors to relax. Somehow, we were to be part of this set-up. The tent crowd, I called them. The hotshots. I was afraid to get my hopes up, but something good was happening.

"Go to wardrobe," one of the men informed Chaim and me. "Not to the one for the extras." He pointed to a white wooden building on the edge of the complex, past the tent. "There are all kinds of uniforms and civilian attire in it. You'll be fitted and shown the different costumes. You'll have to change several times a day sometimes. Go ahead and familiarize yourself with this now. Don't worry about any more scenes today. When you're finished with wardrobe orientation, just come back to the tent and wait to go home."

"Wait. Before you go to wardrobe," another of the stuntmen advised, "follow me to the tent first. You'll meet here at this tent every day to find out what scenes you'll be in and what wardrobe or costume you'll need. So come check it out, and meet some of the actors."

Chaim and I looked at one another with a gleam in our eyes. We almost dared to feel like studs. Sandra stayed a safe distance away, but loosely behind. I was glad she saw all this.

Inside the tent were large upright electrical fans in

the middle of the area. And just like in a Hollywood movie about a set complex, folding chairs were placed, each with an actor's name on the back.

"You will be assigned to this tent area when not in a scene," he said. "Stay out of the actors' way, but be aware of the situation. Stand around near these chairs between scenes and wait to be instructed. Every day, show up with a clean set of clothes. Nothing fancy, just T-shirts and blue jeans, but freshly washed and pressed. Leather shoes or boots—shined. For each special role we use you, we'll send you to wardrobe. There are two wardrobes for you now. The regular extras' wardrobe, and the actors' wardrobe. You'll be bored a lot, but you can't read or play the radio while waiting. Just be patient and alert. Carry on a conversation among yourselves if you desire, but barely above a whisper. This is your life on the set now."

He stared at us to see if we had any questions. After a slight pause he gave a nod and walked away. Chaim and I glanced at one another, then stood silently, hoping all this wasn't a fantasy.

Chapter 7

"I don't know the other four in our stuntman group," Chaim said after we arrived back to our room that night. "I don't know where all these extras come from. There's only a handful here at the hostel. There's the airmen and soldiers from the military bases. There are Korean extras from bases and local villages. But where do all the others come from? Everyone wants to be in a movie, and people come from out of the woodwork." He looked at me with a grin. "That's what you say, isn't it? Like insects come out from the woodwork. It fits."

"The other four are Australians, in our group of stuntmen extras," I replied. "I was curious myself. While we were waiting to board a bus this afternoon, I asked one of them."

"Where was I then?" Chaim asked me. "I was with you all day. I never got to talk to any of them."

"You were talking to Sunshine most of the time. I didn't talk to any of them very much, but they're in the Australian special forces and get time off sometimes."

"That explains why they are so physically fit," Chaim mused.

"I admire them," I said. "I like Australians anyway. They are sort of the Texans of the British world. I almost immigrated to Australia while I was in college. My undergrad days. But I went on to grad school instead. I'm in this part of the world now. Australia is still pretty far away, but at least due south now, from this end of the Pacific Ocean where we are."

"Australians are rather obnoxious," Chaim replied. " 'Cheeky' is the word they use. They are often cheeky bastards, for certain."

"I like these words like 'cheeky,' " I said with a laugh. "I like the Brits, too. I often wish we were still part of the British Empire. I like that we're America and all, but I still wish it was more like Canada and Australia. Independent but with that familial tie."

"The Brits helped us form our country," Chaim explained. "The Balfour Declaration. But they soon backed off. They were afraid to lose their Middle East possessions, with all the Arab nationalism going on. And their overland link to India through the Middle East. But still, if it hadn't been for the Balfour Declaration, we may not have gotten the momentum to pull off the mass immigration to Palestine for the Jews."

"History is so complex," I commented. "Yeah, the Brits came up with the Balfour Declaration, but also the White Paper that was pro-Arab. Then blocked further Jewish immigration all they could while they administered the mandate."

"It was too late by the time they produced the White Paper," Chaim said. "They let the genie out of the bottle with the mandate and couldn't put the genie back in. After Hitler, not to mention two thousand years of subjugation, we Jews weren't going to be denied anymore. Jews were already living in Palestine, and Palestine was mostly desert and sparsely settled. With the desperate Jewish immigrants from Germany and eastern Europe, there was going to be a Jewish state for certain. I'm not a religious person, but it seemed ordained by God."

"Ben Gurion said Israel was a miracle." I thought for a moment. "No, he said it better than that. Very poetically."

"His words were," Chaim reinforced, "in order 'to be a realist, you must believe in miracles.' "

"Yeah," I said with a smile. "Yeah, that. That was a great way to put things. I love the Israelis for things like that. That spunk and flare."

"We appreciate Americans," Chaim praised. "Not just the Jews in America. But so many Christians too have been so supportive."

"Americans like underdogs."

"I am not sure that is always true. Jews have been underdogs for millennia. There is some support in America for Jews and Israel, but also such a stigma."

"The stigma is there, for sure," I agreed, "but a lot of awe and respect for Jews. The haters hate a lot more groups than Jews. Part of a normal bigotry mindset. I'm talking about the average American, who has a lot of respect for Jews, stigma or not. The bigots just blindly hate. I'm from Texas, and we were taught that Jews were the chosen of God."

"But we don't believe Jesus was the Messiah. So that didn't go so far, then, being God's chosen to whatever Christian."

"Not accepting Jesus as Messiah is your lack with a lot of people, for sure. But there is a guarded respect for Jews, with most."

Chaim looked at me skeptically but did not answer.

"We were talking about Aussies," he finally said.

"And now the chosen people."

"I like doers," I commented. "Somehow it's all tied."

"That's why we're chosen," Chaim said with a sigh. "It was that or die. We couldn't even assimilate. Always stuck in some ghetto. Or the focus of some pogrom. We thought the enlightenment saved us, but then there was the Dreyfuss affair. The enlightened French never accepted Jews when push came to shove, and the Dreyfuss affair exposed it. And many French aided Hitler in Vichy France after he conquered it. We never got beyond being strangers in a strange land in our history. So now we own a sliver of land in the Middle East, still hoping to survive."

"But survive you have. Even before modern Israel came about, you survived for centuries. It's as if you really are chosen."

"But like in *Fiddler On The Roof*, sometimes we wish someone else would be chosen."

"How does it feel for you to be in a movie like the one we're in, then?" I mused. "A movie about a part of history that required so much surviving. The Koreans have really had to survive in history. Everyone has, but this movie is significant about their struggle."

"I can identify with their struggle. That is a blessing about being a Jew. We can sympathize with survival and struggle. So I enjoy the movie in that regard."

"Speaking of *Fiddler On The Roof*, it's my favorite movie. I watch it and it gets the Jewish struggle so out there. It more than tells a story—you can feel the struggle with them in the movie. The story is so Jewish, but anyone can identify with them in the movie. And how when things almost seem to be tolerable, a new decree scatters you out again."

"That's why we need our one sliver of land. A sliver that is mostly desert and one of the few places in the Middle East without any oil."

"But that's good," I analyzed. "Oil would make countries want to take you over more."

"They've got their own oil. They don't need oil as an issue to hate us. But having oil would help us survive better. Make us less dependent. We would have to fight just as hard either way."

"Where would you live if not in Israel, then, Chaim?"

He shook his head.

"I'm not sure. I have thought about it sometimes. My parents were from France. But I am too focused on being an Israeli. We need that desire. We are still building our country. We must still be a refuge for Jews everywhere. I am aware, however, that the Philippines was one of the biggest havens for Jews during the time of Hitler. Thousands fled to the Philippines. Their President, Manuel Quezon, welcomed Jews. He would have taken in more, but the Japanese bombed Pearl Harbor and the war started in this part of the world and that refugee haven ended."

"Can't win," I said sarcastically.

"Seems our fate many times."

"It does make me wonder. There is a fate about the Jews. This chosen-ness thing. It has almost wiped you out several times, but for thousands of years you survived. Like no other in history. It has made you Jews. Now you are scholars and lawyers and doctors and Nobel laureates."

"If it doesn't kill you, it makes you stronger," he said with a smirk.

"Yeah. And now we are here making this movie about the same thing. Survival. It fits."

Chaim thought for a second, then shrugged.

"I'm too busy living out this movie while being an Israeli. It is about Korea's struggle, but I can indeed identify with any struggle."

"Speaking of chosen-ness, Chaim," I said as I focused a serious stare on him. "I've got the hots for Sandra. I want to un-choose you and ask her to move in with me."

A broad smile appeared on his face.

"I suspected this," he replied. "I've already wondered where I may live if such occurred. Sunshine has also. We will talk. We have ideas about who else we might live with."

"That will make things easier for me about Sandra, then. I know she likes me. But that doesn't mean she is ready for me like this."

"Then ask her. I'll find a place."

Chapter 8

"I knew you would be coming to see me tonight," Sandra teased as I walked into her room.

Suddenly, I felt shy. I was sure Sunshine had prepared Sandra for the setting now, after talking to Chaim about my plans, but I felt vulnerable anyway.

"Sandra," I mumbled. "Listen, don't get offended."

"Don't get offended about what?" Her broad grin taunted me, but let me know she seemed ready for the subject at hand. "Did I do something, my dear fellow? What is it we should talk about, Wilson?"

Her playfulness helped me relax. I looked her in the eyes.

"I know we spend a lot of time together and all, both from Texas. But we don't know each other intimately."

She scoped me out while broadening her smile. I felt emboldened and reached to pull her to me, then embraced her. She did not resist.

"I like you, Sandra."

"Yes, well, good. And I like you."

"I used the word 'intimate' because that's what I want from you now. Intimacy."

She raised her arms and placed them gently on my chest with her hands touching my neck.

"Okay," she said straightforwardly. "Tell me about intimacy and us."

"I told Chaim that I want you to move in with me. In this room or mine. You and me."

"Yes, I know," she replied. "And I know Chaim told you how Sunshine and I have talked about restructuring both of our living arrangements. But where did this come from, Wilson? We've been great friends and all, but poof, now this."

"It's beyond just friends, and you know it. And you know what I'm talking about. So let's talk bluntly now. I've behaved myself but was always interested."

"Where will Chaim stay? Not with Sunshine. She likes him, but she doesn't want a relationship with anyone. She told me that in our talks."

"There's an open room," I answered. "Or there will be once Sunshine moves in with someone. There are other girls from Europe here, and that could be arranged."

"Yes, it could."

"So this is what I want. You. You and me. And then go back to Texas together and see what happens."

"See what happens, huh? Well, hmm."

"Yes, I'm ready to see what happens with you and me. Let's endeavor."

"Sunshine and I talked about that, too," she said with a smile. "We talk about a lot of stuff. She saw a spark between us and wondered why neither one of us pursued it. I wondered too. I even fantasized about us. But you've turned into this big movie star on me, and what if I was just becoming a groupie?"

"So you've thought about it too. About us. Good. I felt vibes from you, but I wasn't sure if I was just projecting my own fantasies."

"How long have you felt this way, hot shot?"

"Right from the first, to be honest. When you rescued me at the airport. But I'm a guy. Guys are always on the prowl."

"Yes, ha. Yes, they are. But I couldn't be sure of my own fantasies. Especially with you being such a natural in this movie. Even Matt Jillette's girlfriend flirts with you."

"What are you talking about?" I asked.

"You've been in a couple of scenes with her. And with those other actors in the movie with her reporter group. I don't know their names. But now and then reporters are in the field in a scene. Sometimes she is with them afterwards at the Air Force base, getting to be American again or something. The woman reporter actress in the group is supposedly Matt Jillette's girlfriend."

"That explains it, then," I mused.

"Explains what?"

"She can't act. She doesn't even stand around in a scene well, you know, when the reporters are waiting to take pictures of MacArthur or whoever in a scene. And once when she was supposed to take a picture, she pressed the wrong button and the flashbulb popped out. I figured she had to have someone's favor that mattered."

Sandra let out a laugh. "Well, she fancies you, Wilson. You couldn't tell? So all the more I wasn't sure you were interested in me. You are so warm and friendly to me, but you're just this nice Texan and all, and I'm from Texas with you. So I had some doubts about what was friendly about you and what might be flirtations like I make toward you sometimes while hoping to plant a seed or two."

"I *melt* every time you touch me," I said. "Just placing your hand on my shoulder or fixing my collar when I'm wearing a uniform for a scene."

"Yeah, flirtations," she repeated pointedly.

"So this is all your fault, and now you have to move in with me. Chaim will understand, and so will Sunshine."

"Sunshine already understands. I told you that. She even pushes me about you. That I should make a play for you. I just preferred to take my time and let the hormones talk. Too much going on, and I didn't want to spoil anything."

"So you'll move in with me?"

She nodded emphatically.

"Let me get my stuff," she chirped. "Ah, I forgot. Chaim hasn't been informed of our hormones yet. Not on an official basis, anyway. Beyond normal gossip and fantasy."

"Yes, he has. We've talked. He can move out in five minutes. We're all traveling light, you know."

Sandra laughed, then leaned up to kiss me. I kissed her back.

"It's what I want," she said.

I nodded and gave a self-confident, macho smile in celebration.

"I have feelings for you, Sandra."

She gave a serious look directly into my eyes, then pulled me toward her to kiss me on the lips.

Chapter 9

"Our first night together," I celebrated as I lay next to Sandra on the single-width mattress we had commandeered from the hostel storage room.

She wrapped her arm around mine and laid her head next to my shoulder.

"Glad we put the mattress next to the wall," she said with a chuckle. "I need it for support when you turn. You seem ready to fall off, on your side, and so you push me sometimes. I'm scared you're going to smash me."

"I like to snuggle," I concurred, "but I need to turn on my side or back, too. I'll get used to it. I haven't fallen off yet. We're on the floor, and the mattress is thin, so it won't hurt if I do, but I need some sleep."

"How are we going to do it?" she asked wickedly.

"Do what?" I asked as if I didn't know.

"Right. Sure. What, huh? You know the hell what. There's all these people around us. They'll hear our heavy breathing and moans of ecstasy. That's bad enough. But if we get very wild, we'll both be bouncing on the floor."

"A three-inch mattress isn't going to create a bounce. Even if we fell."

I was dying to see her expression as we talked, but the windowless room was pitch dark.

"So are you propositioning me?" I asked.

"It's not a proposition, sweets. It's a road map to our evolving relationship. We're not lying in the two army cots nearby for a reason, you know. Cuddling is simply foreplay. This is the Age of Aquarius, isn't it?"

"Age of who?" I asked. "That was a millennium ago. Age of Aquarius? Where've you been?"

"You know what I'm talking about. We're here together now because this is where the sixties brought us. Even us Texas hicks take free love for granted these days."

"You're interesting, ya know," I said with a laugh.

"It gets more interesting than this."

"Listen, Sandra. I was going to go slow with you. I already lured you into my cobweb here. I wanted to give you time to adjust before I pounced."

"I do need to adjust a bit, but I'm not going to be shy about it. We're going to make love, and we both know it. I don't feel like being shy about it."

I had to think what to say next. I liked her boldness, but it took me aback.

"Now that I've said all that," she continued, "I'm not ready to go any further tonight. I like you next to me. And I like that we are open about things together. But I still need to get used to us. Bold us, I mean. Let the hormones tease us some more. I want it to be natural and uninhibited. The longing will prepare us."

I felt a surge of emotion. I propped myself up by an arm, then touched her face with my fingertips. She reached to touch my face also, then leaned to kiss me.

"Shut the door, Wilson," she coaxed me. "I changed my mind. I want you now. Turn the fan on high before you get back in bed. With the door shut it will be hot, excuse the pun, and we'll need the fan, plus it will make some noise."

I got up excitedly and closed the door slowly to minimize the squeak. I felt scandalous at what I knew our neighbors must be thinking about the stillness we disturbed. It surprised me that I cared.

Cautiously, I made my way back to our bed on the floor. Sandra touched my arm and led me back next to her. She then placed my hand on her now-bare breasts.

"Just hold me for a moment," she instructed. "Take off your clothes, and let's just hold each other. Skin on skin."

She kissed me softly.

"We know what's going to happen," she whispered seductively into my ear while she kissed it. "And it begins now."

Chapter 10

"You belong in movies, Wilson," Sandra said to me between scenes. "You look like a Hollywood guy. Tall, muscular, brown hair, good looks. And, lo and behold, you can act. Out of three thousand extras, you outdid all of us, and they're still using you."

"You haven't gotten your chance yet," I said to her sympathetically.

"Well, they looked around and chose you. I was even standing close to you when they did."

"But this is a guy movie," I consoled. "War and all."

"They still chose you and Chaim to be with the stuntmen sometimes. You look the part and you act the part. They sought you out. They checked you out."

"I don't act," I replied, trying to appear humble.

"Yes, you do. And you've been discovered. I know what you mean, though, it is a bit part. But you're part of the stuntmen and are used more than the rest of us. And you've been in scenes with Roy Holland. Sometimes without the other stuntmen."

"So who is Roy Holland?" I asked. "I never heard of him."

"Me either. But I was told by some of the extras that he's been in some daytime soap operas. I don't know which ones, not that I would know them anyway. But he's one of the actors in this movie, and you just filmed a scene in a foxhole with him this afternoon."

"It was fun," I replied as I thought about it. "Boring but fun. We stood around half the afternoon just to get in one scene. I got to act again, too, quote unquote. Holland looked up at the sky and said there's aircraft on the way and how he hoped it was ours. I looked up toward the distance and pretended I was concerned but hopeful."

"See, Wilson? See? You *are* an actor. You gave that explanation some depth. You didn't just look up in the sky, following a lead of some sort. You weren't even just concerned. You were concerned and hopeful too. It's a bit part, but it has to be authentic. You're thinking about all of this. Picturing it. Relating to it."

I took a deep breath. She made me feel good. I wanted to believe her. Sandra was my lover, but also my fan.

Chaim walked quickly toward me.

"Listen, Freddy is calling for us," he warned. "We are needed."

I kissed Sandra on the cheek and made my way to the set nearby.

"Quiet on the set," I heard Freddy bark into his megaphone. "Quiet on the set. Quiet, please. Quiet. We have much work to do."

He began to look around impatiently.

"You two," Freddy called out to Chaim and me. "They need you on the set. Quickly."

Chaim and I ran toward him.

"Yo," I answered slightly out of breath. "Chaim and I are here."

"Yo," Freddy mimicked with a laugh. "You must be from the South."

"Texas is part of the South," I replied.

"I thought you were all cowboys," he joked further. "Listen, you seem to be working out fine with our stuntmen. They're in a scene now in the village. The stuntmen that you work with are, I mean. We don't need you today as an extra here. We need you as special soldiers, Marines, in a scene with our professional stuntmen. Can you please proceed to wardrobe so they can fit you? The wardrobe for stuntmen. Then proceed to the next scene."

Chaim and I looked at one another, showing the pleasure these instructions induced.

"I like working with the stuntmen," I said as we jogged to wardrobe. "There is always something going on in their scenes, and some of it includes us. We get recognition for it, too."

"Yes, Wilson. Exactly. This is why I told you to stick close to me. But now the directors and stuntmen go straight to you as much if not more than they do me. This is what I was saying that first night we met, though. For nobodies, we seem to be on the make-it trail."

The make-it trail. Exactly where I wanted to be.

"Over here," Freddy yelled at us as we returned in gear from wardrobe. "Texas boy, Israeli," he barked further. "Get on the truck with the rest of the stuntmen. We've been waiting for you. That is a luxury, to have to wait on you."

As I boarded the truck, it dawned on me that Freddy had called me "boy." Every macho fiber in me rustled from the realization of his slander.

"Where are we going?" I asked Chaim as we bounced along the potholed highway. Chaim looked at me blankly as his answer.

For an hour we drove, until we came upon sand dunes. I could see no signs of ocean but decided we must be near a beach somewhere.

"Depart, please," Freddy ordered. "We are late in arriving. It will be dark before we finish filming unless we are efficient with this scene."

Freddy studied us before delivering more orders.

"All the stuntmen extras," he spewed. "You are needed at the encampment just beyond the large sand dune in front of you. There will be Korean enemy, bivouacked, for you to attack. Stuntmen must form with the rest of the soldiers for this scene. I need the group of you from the truck just now to form loosely. You will be at a jog. Look determined and focused. You must surprise the enemy. They do not expect UN forces in this area."

We formed as we were instructed.

"Good," Freddy said approvingly. "Very good. So now. You will run straight ahead toward the director on top of the sand dune in front of you."

He pointed at a huge wall-like sand dune that was easily a story high and as wide as half a city block.

"He is your marker to focus upon," Freddy continued. "All of you are physically able to run this. Not too fast, so that you will have breath remaining to charge the unsuspecting enemy. Charge up the sand dune the assistant director is on, and he will wave you farther to where you should go. We have camera and equipment along the way. When the assistant director on the sand dune signals with his hand flashing downward as if for a racing car, you are to point your rifles from your chest area and begin to yell. We will collect our scenes all throughout. The enemy will be surprised and you will be ruthless. You have fake bayonets on your rifles, so do not stab the enemy even though these bayonets are plastic, with a weak joint attaching them to the rifle, ready to break on contact. They still can do damage to someone, even though dull and weak. So do not make such an accident. We will stop the filming before you would physically pierce anyone. The enemy will be frightened and in disarray. You will be victorious, and we will film your victory and celebration. We will do staged close-ups as you fight later on. For now, just concentrate on the charge."

This was like any game of play "war" back home while we were growing up as kids. Except more organized. And on film. Perfect.

I barely had breath to scream after running toward and then up the sand dune. I thought how to make my part more dramatic, much like I did in my first scene as an unknown extra.

"Kill," I snarled as I approached my prey past the sand dune.

My pretended victim was startled and showed fear. I could tell that was not an act on his part. I spooked him and felt powerful for it.

"Commie bastard," I shouted further.

My victim froze. This was counter-productive, I decided. I slowed my pace and eased the menacing look on my face. The Korean then regrouped and ran away on cue.

"That was a hard day's work," I said to Chaim as we rode back on the truck to Pusan. It was twilight now, with only shadowy remnants of daylight remaining.

"We had such encounters in the Sinai," Chaim told me along the way. "We trained there just before I took this leave to travel. To charge just now against a fake enemy brought back memories for me." He smiled as he looked at me. "I had more fun this time and got paid more."

"I would love to be Israeli," I said to him.

He shook his head and looked the other way.

"I am a proud Israeli. But I don't love the wars or training. It is duty. It is to stay alive. That is what I was thinking as we charged just now. Even on my travel excursion, here I am charging the enemy. It makes me think there is nothing else in life but to survive. How does one escape such a fate?"

Chapter 11

"So who sang this?" a newly arrived American asked back at the hostel grounds after another day of filming.

He began to strum his guitar, then to sing.

"Ah, my goodness, yes, who was that?" Sunshine mused aloud after he finished singing. "I know the song. I cannot for the life of me remember who sang it."

"You're from Sweden," the Brit in the group teased. "You're not supposed to know."

"No, the Swedes know this stuff," I said to take up for Sunshine. "This new rock group out of Sweden, ABBA, knows every song, and they sing and speak with no accent. Just like Sunshine here. How the hell do y'all not have an accent? I expected you to go around telling us about the Sveedishe meataballsuh, but y'all speak better than I do. The Dutch, too."

"You're from Texas," the Brit teased further. "Everyone speaks better English than you."

"Thank you for your compliment, Wilson," the Dutch girl in our contingent replied. "We do speak quite good English in Holland, I must say. We are such a small country, and just across the channel from England. No one speaks our Nordic dialect besides us in Holland. We must speak English or die, I think."

"But Wilson," Sunshine broke back in. "You are

the star of the group. You and Chaim, our Israeli. Such big shots. I wanted to get your autographs, after all your scenes today on the set. Maybe I will, while you are still nobodies."

"That's right," the Nepalese said with a laugh. "While you are still nobodies. One of the nobodies here at our hostel of nobody extras."

"It is like a hostel of extras, isn't it?" the Brit seconded.

"So who sang 'You Are My Sunshine'?" the American with the guitar asked again. "That was the song just now, in honor of our glorious Swede by the same name."

"Jimmie Davis," I answered.

"Who is that?" a girl from L.A. asked.

"Yes, Jimmie Davis, yes, him," Sunshine confirmed. "Wasn't he a singing cowboy?"

"A bit," I agreed. "Mostly a singer, though, and he was governor of Louisiana, too."

"Louisiana," the Brit said with a bite. "They hate the black people, don't they?"

"Like in Texas," the Nepalese mused. "Why do you hate all these people of a different culture and race?"

Everyone looked at me for the spot I was in.

"I don't hate you," I said with a smile.

"Only because you are one of us now," he replied. "But back in Texas, I am a ghetto."

"The ghetto is where outcasts in America live," I corrected. "There was racism while I was growing up, for sure. And many of our schools segregated. That seems a long time ago to me now."

"Are we going to have a civil rights protest here?"

Sunshine asked. "Wilson and Sandra are both from Texas and are now here in Korea with us, and I see no problem in how they act or behave. We can say scandal about anyone, somehow. We have a good time. Do not spoil things."

"All because I sang 'You Are My Sunshine,' " the American with the guitar snickered.

"Yes," Sunshine said, "because of me. My song. About me. About sunshine, you know. I have this beautiful song named for me and now we talk politics. Not even politics about the Communists, but about Selma, Alabama."

"My God," I sighed, "y'all know everything about back home, don't you?"

"Because America is so significant," Sunshine praised. "No one knows enough about Scandinavia to criticize us. So let's sing some more."

"What's the owner think of all this singing?" Sandra asked. "We get a little loud."

"He sings right along when he's out here with us," Chaim commented.

"Why are not your bosoms more big, Sunshine?" the Nepalese asked, directing us to a different subject. "All these stories about sex and sex goddesses in Sweden we hear."

Everyone laughed and stared at Sunshine.

"Yes," the Brit came in, "Sandra has bigger bosoms than Sunshine. But since we're on the subject, Sunshine has very nice bosoms."

Sunshine broke into a smile and looked down at her breasts. She tugged on her blouse to expand her breasts more outwardly to the fore.

"We are getting too much attention, dear ones," she

said looking down at her endowment as she did so. She looked back at us. "Can we not sing a bit more now? Singing is so much better than politics or sex."

"Nothing is better than sex," the Brit said as he let out a giggle.

"Defend your girlfriend, Wilson," Chaim insisted. "He talks about Sandra's big bosoms."

I let out a laugh and looked the other way. I pictured my friends back home and how they might respond to my life now. As exciting as it was to be in a Hollywood movie during the day, the real joy was our get-togethers at night. I wanted everyone back home to be here now with me and behold.

Chapter 12

"We need one of you to be in a foxhole with Roy Holland," the lead stuntman told the extras among the group one morning. "You will audition for that part. It is not a big part, but what it means, in particular, is that the one we select will now be put with the cast of actors on a regular basis. You will have small roles at times with some of these actors. We only need one of you, so that is why there will be an audition. Nothing fancy, the roles won't require fancy. But we need authentic. That's what will get you the part. Which of you is the most authentic? You'll get extra pay, too. Instead of the steady thirty-five dollars a day, you'll get ninety."

I felt my stomach tighten. Right here, right now, I had to prove myself. I thought a moment about the situation, including my tenseness and how badly I wanted to be the one selected. I exuded nervousness. Calm down, I lectured myself. But not too calm, I decided. I needed the focus. Then, suddenly, I felt a surge of confidence. I reminded myself how I already had been around Roy Holland as part of the stuntmen.

"Everyone line up," the head stuntman instructed. "You're in an open field, and the enemy is behind the next hill. They are firing at you with artillery. When I clap my hands, I want all of you to be hit and fall down dead. Are you picturing it?"

Don't overact, I analyzed. *Be convincing, but don't*

overact.

The head stuntman walked behind us.

"Listen for the clap of my hand," he repeated. "That is artillery and you are hit. Fatally hit."

There was silence for a moment, then the sound of the stuntman's clap.

I'm hit, I told myself while grimacing, eyes flinching. I jerked my neck and collapsed backward, lips pursed, with my rigid arms and hands out slightly. My knees buckled as I fell to the ground, then lay motionless and limp.

I could hear footsteps among us.

"Very good," one of the professional stuntmen said. "Now get up. Then, one at a time, beginning on the left side as I face you, I want you to yell out, 'We're being bombarded.' "

I was fourth in the row of extras. I reminded myself yet again not to overact.

I was curious how the three before me would do their line, but was afraid to be influenced by them. I had to do it my way. In my own voice and demeanor. The guy just before me was so melodramatic, I had to put him out of my head to regain my bearings.

"Okay, you," the head stuntman instructed me.

I must be a Paul Revere warning of danger, I coached myself, but someone still in control.

"We're being bombarded," I said forcefully while squinting my eyes in alarm.

There was silence after my line. Then the next extra after me began.

Chaim was the last of us to audition. He seemed forced. I was pulling for him, but at the same time was glad he blew it. One less to worry about.

The stuntmen again talked briefly among themselves after we all yelped out our line. The head stuntman then walked over and stood in front of me.

"You're the Texan?" he asked me. "Right?"

I nodded and showed some of the confidence flowing inside me.

"Okay, then. I think your name is Wilson."

I nodded again.

"Follow me. I'm going to take you over to where they are shooting now. I will place you with the actor Roy Holland. You will be in a foxhole with him. Similar to what you've done before. I'll take you first to wardrobe. You will be a Marine corporal. I'm not sure if you will have a speaking part, but you outdid the others in the action and the speaking just now. You'll do fine no matter what. When you've been given your uniform, go to one of the latrines to change into it. It will be cramped there and stink, but you're still a nobody, so that's how it is for you still. After you've changed clothing, I'll take you to Roy Holland."

I tried to act normal as I walked along, but my head was spinning, and I wanted to howl in celebration. I glanced back after a few yards to check out Chaim, who smiled approvingly my way.

"When we get to wardrobe," the stuntman informed, "I'll make sure the girl gets you the right articles. It will include a cartridge belt. I'll help you put it all on correctly. Behave yourself around the girl in wardrobe. That's not a threat. And not because she's good-looking, which she is, but she's the producer's daughter. She's an idiot, but we owed a favor. Well, Matt Jillette did. I have to make sure she gives you a Marine uniform and not a tuxedo, since she's so out of it. I'm being facetious, I think. Anyway, for your own good, stay away from her. She'll think you a hunk. But she is trouble. That's my warning about it and why. But it's up to you."

We walked to a wooden building just across from the tent where the actors relaxed between scenes. As we entered wardrobe, I saw table after table of clothing items including military gear, hats, shoes, as well as furniture pieces. The blonde-haired girl in charge was behind the front table.

"This is the guy I was telling you about," the stuntman said to the girl. "I hope you have all the Marine gear I asked for. I wasn't sure of his size because we hadn't picked anyone yet, but I gave you a couple of estimates. Is any of his gear ready for him?"

"Yes, just a minute," she answered. "Let me show you. It's the pieces here to the side on this little coffee table."

She walked over to retrieve the gear.

"Here," she said. "I put the clothing items in three stacks. The cartridge belt and rifle and other military pieces are next to it, since they don't have to be a particular size."

"Wait a minute," the stuntman said. "One of the piles of clothing has a sailor's jacket in it. This man will be a Marine."

"Well, I couldn't find a jacket the same size as the other clothing. The sailor's jacket is the same size as the T-shirt and the collared shirt. It's the same color."

"But it has upside down chevrons on it. That's Navy. It matters. Not just in macho pride stuff, but for authenticity."

"Yes, it does," she said with a sigh. "Sorry. My

goodness, what was I thinking?"

"Never mind," the stuntman said with a huff. "That's not his size anyway. Give me the stack of clothes on the right. That's for bigger guys. We'll try that on. We'll make do."

He turned to me.

"Just try this fatigue jacket on," he instructed as he handed it to me. "If it fits, we'll take this bunch of clothing. Try the rest on later. If something doesn't fit, we can always come back."

I was wearing a T-shirt and put the jacket over it.

"Good," the stuntman said. "Good enough. The military is famous for not having clothing that fits well. Your arm length is a tad too long for the sleeves, but that's barely noticeable. You'll be in a group most of the time anyway. This is a war zone and not a fashion show."

"What do I do with my old gear already assigned me today?"

"Bring it along and turn everything in at the end of the day. What you had before is Army gear. This is Marine. I'm not trying to insult your intelligence. I don't know what you know. But turn it all in at the end of each day, and we'll go over what pertains to you on a daily basis and have it sorted for you for the next day. Today you're a Marine like Roy Holland."

He looked at the girl and said, "We'll take it," then abruptly turned to leave.

The girl picked up the pile of clothes and handed them to me. She then handed me the combat gear. I struggled to handle it all, then rushed to catch up with my cohort. I was feeling more like a somebody with each step back to the set.

Chapter 13

"I need a Marine in this scene," Matt Jillette bellowed.

Freddy looked my way.

"You. You there. The Roy Holland double. Go to wardrobe. Tell the girl we need wardrobe for a Marine. We previously informed her you would be coming. Change into your uniform there and return here. Time is of the essence. We are waiting on your return to begin filming again."

This sounded important. Maybe even a part for me and not just as another extra in a mob.

"Matt Jillette sent me here," I told the girl as I caught my breath. "I have a part as a Marine in the next scene. They are waiting on me now."

"Yes," she replied. "I have your uniform prepared. Here. Take these items. You can change in the closet behind you. You don't have to go to the latrine to change anymore."

I was anxious as I struggled to change. It seemed forever to take off my combat boots and then put them back on after getting into my new wardrobe, knowing they were waiting on me. I rushed back to the set, and it was as if time stood still while I was gone. They had waited solely for me. I could see the impatience on everyone's faces.

"What is that?" Matt Jillette groaned. "Good grief.

That's the wrong uniform. That is a combat uniform. This is a scene on a boat. You even had a part. But we must have the correct uniform. We need someone in what they call class B, the office uniform. We don't have time to wait for this clown to change again. Get this joker out of here."

In disgust, Matt Jillette looked around the set.

"You there," he called out to an extra already in a Marine class B uniform. "Come here. You'll do. You don't look the part with that hair, but it's a movie. We'll go with it. Better than wearing the wrong uniform."

The extra that was chosen in my place indeed had bushy hair intruding on the nape of his neck, as well as long sideburns past his earlobes. I was fit to be tied with all this. I not only lost a closeup scene due to this bimbo in wardrobe, but I wanted to punch the director, too. A joker, he called me. It didn't hurt my feelings, but it disgusted me all the more in its callousness and ego.

Roy Holland sat in his chair and looked the other way from me as I left the actors' area. I wondered why I expected a conciliatory expression from him. A joker is a joker, and that's my place here, it assured me. I did not hide my disdain as I made my way to the crowd of extras to find Sandra.

"You had a part," she said to me sympathetically as she stroked my cheek. "Now, just like that, you're out."

I thought to be philosophical and brave, but increased the sneer I wore instead.

"I feel like punching him out," I said. "I won't, but I wish God wasn't looking."

"Who?" she asked. "Matt Jillete? This is Hollywood. That's how they do things."

"I'd like to show him how Texans do things."

I looked at her and absorbed how she hurt for me. Suddenly, that was all that mattered.

"There'll be other roles," I moaned. "To hell with this."

I kissed her softly on her lips. Soft, moist lips that I wouldn't have gotten just now if I was making that scene instead. That helped soothe the pain. I wrapped my arm inside her elbow while we walked back toward the tent.

"Sit in my chair, Sandra." I beckoned her.

She looked around cautiously. "Won't you get in trouble?"

"Maybe. We'll find out. I'll stand next to you until the next scene is ready to start."

My emotions were exploding inside me, set off by my encounter with the director of the movie but channeled to the most precious person in my life anymore as I stood beside her.

"Sandra," I said softly as I turned to look at her.

She looked at me as if anticipating my feelings.

"I love you," I said nervously. "I know it's awkward to say it like this and here on the set, too. But I can't hold it anymore. It seems trite to hold this inside for you. It's not enough to have feelings or affection. I love you. I mean, I love you."

"I feel so awkward, Wilson. To hear all this and to be where I can't respond to you like I want. Like I need. But I love you too. I should have told you already. Things are going so fast, though. I've been trying to cope. But I love you, Wilson. We're at a new level now."

I nodded. A simple nod to finalize the drama I felt.

Before we could continue further release of our emotions, I saw the head stuntman coming our way.

"You won't need your helmet this afternoon," he informed me in a very businesslike tone when he arrived. "Check it back into wardrobe. Your cartridge belt, too. We'll still be in field fatigues, though, so you'll need to keep wearing what you have on."

The anticlimax of his announcement humored me after all the intensity of emotion in my life now.

"Try not to cuss out the wardrobe girl there," the stuntman said as an afterthought. "I'm sorry about what happened with you. To take up for Matt, he doesn't have time for mistakes or to blame. He's got to keep things going. It's life. It'll happen again in some way. But more good will happen, so it evens out."

I nodded with a half-smile. I felt able to handle anything Hollywood could dish out.

Sandra walked with me back to wardrobe, as much from curiosity about this girl who had ruined my Hollywood life as to savor our new commitment to one another. Any animosity I had toward the girl in wardrobe was pushed away. The words my colleague had shared resonated as I approached her. More good will happen, he said. More good had already happened, in fact. And more good would follow. I could feel it.

"I won't need this helmet or the cartridge belt," I told the girl as I placed them on the counter in front of her.

"All right, then," she responded. "Did they change their mind? You never know what's going to happen on the set."

"Wilson," I heard a voice behind me say.

I turned to see that it was Chaim.

74

"Come now. Roy Holland needs you. Just come. You will be with him in a truck. The troops are being transferred to another battle scene, and you have to be in the transport to that scene. Come. They won't wait long. The uniform you are wearing now will be good. They told me that. Forget the new uniform after all."

Maybe I should thank the wardrobe girl and pretend she knew what she was doing after all, I thought to myself. I ran so fast I left Sandra behind. I turned quickly to wait, but she motioned me onward.

When the driver of the truck spotted me, he jammed the gears and began going forward. My momentum from running carried me easily onto the truck bed in one leap as I grabbed the overhead bar at the back for support.

"That was great, Wilson," Roy Holland said to me as he clapped me on the back. "I don't think they were filming just now, but I wish they were. Your leap onto the truck has got to be in the movie. We'll get you in other shots somehow. Can't waste you on just foxhole scenes."

The stuntman's encouragement from before came to mind. Things indeed even out. And like we often said back in Texas, *You make your own luck.*

Chapter 14

"Why don't you sing something, Wilson?" Sunshine asked me at the hostel one night. "Everyone has sung us something except you."

"You haven't sung anything, Sunshine," I replied. "Neither has Sandra."

"Leave me out of this, Wilson," Sandra said as she squirmed.

"Give Wilson the guitar," Sunshine insisted. "He's the guy in all these movie scenes among us. What other talents does he possess? He may be a singing cowboy, for all we know."

"Give it to Chaim," I instructed. "He's Israeli. Jewish. They sing spirited music. '*Hava Nagila*' or whatever. You see them in movies dancing and clapping. Here's our chance."

"I don't sing, and I don't play the guitar," Chaim said with a growl.

"Wilson's right," Sunshine insisted. "That's neat stuff, Chaim. Bottle dances and such. Strut your stuff for us here."

"I'm Israeli, but this is not *Fiddler On The Roof*. I don't know how to sing or play guitar, and you will regret you made me sing, if I give in. Which I will not. I don't know how to do any bottle dance, either. Wilson knows how to play the guitar. I never heard him, but he told me his father sang in church and how he learned how to play guitar. Bother Wilson, not me."

"I'm not going to sing anything, Sunshine," I groaned.

"Yeah, Wilson," the Brit said as he handed me the guitar.

"And what makes you think I can play the guitar?" I answered.

"Because you said you could, one night. You showed me how to form an A minor. I don't play minor chords, but I needed it on that John Lennon song, and you showed me."

"That doesn't mean I can sing."

The Brit responded by handing me the guitar forcefully.

I took the guitar as I nodded my head, accepting their demands.

"Key of E," the Brit said as I formed it on the guitar neck.

I acknowledged that it was and began to pound out a rhythm, then began to sing.

"I spent all my life
Listening all my life
Now deep inside there ain't no pity for you
Ain't no pity for you."

In unison the others at the hostel began to clap their hands to the beat.

"And I spent all my life
Humbled by all your might
Just making way to let your ego pass through
I made it so easy for you."

"Hey, man, go, baby," Sunshine praised.

All in the group cheered my performance by song's end. I tried staying straight-faced as I handed back the guitar to the Brit, but soon began smirking. I was glad they'd dragged me into this endeavor after all.

"My God, Wilson," the Dutch girl swooned. "You can do anything. You're like some superman among us. The leading Hollywood among us on the set. And this long tall Texan that you are. What are we going to dream up next for you?"

"Superman," Sunshine said with a gleam. "Yes, Superman fits our Texan here."

"Who sang that song?" the Brit asked. "I never heard it before."

"John Lennon," I responded.

"No, he didn't," he replied. "No, he didn't. Somewhere I would have heard it. I know I don't know every song he ever sang, but no. I would have heard that before, somewhere. A song like that, anyway."

"Buddy Holly," I answered this time.

"No, no," the Brit answered back forcefully. "I know most of his songs too. Who sang it? Seriously. Who?"

"I did," I answered.

"The hell, you say," the new Frenchman among us exclaimed.

"So you are a singer, you are saying," Sunshine cut in. "What do you mean, you sang it?"

"No, I'm not a singer, but I wrote it. You asked who sang it, so I said I did."

"You write music?" Sunshine asked, amazed.

"I grew up on a farm in Texas. A lot of Texans sing and write. I gave it a try when I was in high school, and it's easy to write a song. It might not be good, but so what."

"Well, that was great," Sunshine praised further.

"Speaking of Buddy Holly, it had a Buddy Holly sound to it. He's from Texas, right?"

I nodded that he was. "Lubbock," I replied. "Out in West Texas. I grew up in South Texas, but my parents were from West Texas, so I liked him for that. I was a big Beatles fan later on. They were influenced a lot by Buddy Holly. I particularly liked John Lennon and read how he patterned after Buddy Holly more than anyone. I think I read that. Anyway, speaking of John Lennon, just before I came to Korea I heard him sing a song he wrote called 'Working Class Heroes.' It sounded very much like a Bob Dylan song. And in fact, he said he wanted to sound like Dylan on that song. All the hoopla Dylan was getting for his folk songs? And Lennon said if Bob Dylan can do that, so can I, and he wrote 'Working Class Heroes' as a response to prove it. And I got uppity when I heard John Lennon say all that and decided if Bob Dylan can do that, and John Lennon can do that in response, by God, so can I. So I came up with 'Ain't No Pity,' the song you just heard."

"We've got to get this song in the movie we're doing now," the Brit came in. "Right here, our moment. How are we going to get Matt Jillette to listen to Superman sing this and then get him wanting to put it in a movie?"

"Boy, that's ambition," Sunshine countered. "But yeah, how will we manage this? But you're right. Wilson here, Superman, is one of us, so it almost makes it feel like we're doing it for us too. We'll be watching this movie someday with our grandkids and tell them the story of how we knew Wilson the superman from Texas and watched him become a movie star right in front of us."

She then looked at Sandra, who sat near me.

"So how, Sandra?" Sunshine mused. "How are we going to get your boyfriend here in the movie with that song?"

Sandra blushed as she grinned my way.

"Listen," I interrupted, "I appreciate this and all, and if the opportunity presents itself, I'd love to do this. Matt Jillette, though, doesn't have time for us nobodies. I'm glad to be allowed to hang around Roy Holland and all the stuntmen and all. But I don't want to push my luck."

"We'll push your luck, Superman," Sunshine said happily. "This is fun. This whole movie is fun, especially the after-movie times, like now."

"Don't, Sunshine." I squirmed. "Seriously, were there to be some kind of opening, I'll try to maneuver, but I love what I'm doing and don't want to be greedy. Or pushy."

"Sing another one," Sunshine coaxed. "Doesn't have to be one of yours."

I thought for a moment, then began to strum the guitar and sing.

"What was that?" Sandra asked after I finished the song. "I've heard it before, somewhere."

"You're from Texas," I responded. "You may have come across it growing up even if you don't like hillbilly music. Jimmie Rodgers, the singing brakeman. From back in the depression. He was from Mississippi but spent his last years out in Lubbock."

"My God," Sunshine said. "Lubbock again. I didn't know so much came out of this place, wherever it is. West Texas or wherever?"

"I love these songs," I said longingly as I thought

back to my younger days.

"Do they still have singing cowboys?" Sunshine asked, looking at me.

"You're still pushing this agenda, Sunshine," I said, loving the flattery.

"She needs to," the French guy interrupted. "Yes, you will be our project. And for ourselves too, just like Sunshine said."

"No, they don't do singing cowboy stuff anymore," I replied.

"Okay, then," Sunshine intervened yet again. "So that I get to say I used to room with Superman's girlfriend before they were an item, here we are in a more modern setting of the singing cowboys. You'll be in a foxhole, but during a lull in the fighting, while you're bored, you start singing. We need a guitar in that foxhole somehow. Maybe Matt Jillette can arrange that."

"A harmonica," the Brit suggested. "You can put a harmonica in your pocket or pack, Superman. Out it comes and then start singing about good old Texas and the coyotes. That's cowboy suggestive. So there. A way around anything."

"And Matt Jillette is going to accept these marvelous proposals," I scoffed, "when they are already spending millions of dollars for Hollywood stars."

"All the more reason," Sunshine countered. "Just one scene. One little foxhole scene of the troops, the backbone of the army. Missing his mother. Real corny stuff to break up a war movie and make it to where we can all identify. A human side to the warriors."

"I'm not paying you any agent fees, Sunshine," I said with a chuckle. "And since you aren't an agent anyway, Matt Jillette isn't going to buy anything any of y'all suggest. This is fun and all, but hey, give me a break."

"To hell with you," the French guy snickered. "This is our ego trip, not yours. Mind your own business. I think in Texas you say, 'You can kiss my ass.' Well, Mr. Texan, just kiss our ass."

I laughed appreciatively, as much to end the subject as to enjoy the moment. I then looked at Sandra.

"Enough for one night, don't you think?" I asked her.

"This is fun, Wilson," she replied. "And with everybody here in your corner, what if we can present some opportunity for you?"

"Aw, you too?" I moaned. "Come on, kiddo. Let me keep my feet on the ground before I start believing all this stuff."

"Believe it," Sunshine said.

"Yes, believe it," the Brit reinforced. "But go seduce your girlfriend. We buttered her up for you."

Chapter 15

"Have you seen Sandra?" I asked Sunshine. "Why isn't she with you?"

"She was here just a minute ago. I wasn't paying attention. Nothing ever happens in our boring little world, and I didn't notice her gone."

"There wasn't much going on in my world either, until now," I commented. "We got lulled to sleep. I hope opportunity doesn't have a quota."

"You mean it only knocks once?" she asked.

"That's the quota I heard about."

"Did you see Sandra?" Sunshine asked the Dutch girl standing a few feet away.

"No," she answered. "She was just here. Why? Do you need her for something?"

"Listen," I said, showing frustration. "There's a scene coming up. This assistant director, the Greek guy I talk about now and then, he's sort of in charge of me. He told me we're going to get on a truck soon and go to a nearby town. They need a dozen women or so in this scene, and he asked me to round y'all up. I don't want you to miss your chance by looking for Sandra, but can you help me find her for a couple of minutes first? If we don't find her in a couple of minutes, go on without us."

"Sandra," Sunshine began to shout.

"Sandra," the other girls in our group called out.

"Sandra," other extras bellowed on our behalf. "Sandra!"

"Nothing," I groaned. "Nothing. How can this be happening?"

"There she is," Sunshine said pointing. "She's heading toward wardrobe. Maybe she's looking for you."

"I'll get her," I replied. "All you girls go to those trucks in front of us. I'll get her and we'll meet you there."

I ran frantically toward Sandra, elbowing my way through a mob at times.

"There you are," Sandra said to me as I approached her. "You're all winded. Where have you been?"

"Looking for you," I answered. "They're getting ready to call out for women in a scene. Ten or twenty, even. I wanted to make sure you didn't miss out."

"Yeah, that's where I was going to head after I found you and the girls," she said. "I didn't want you to get left out. Chaim told me about this scene coming up. I wanted to check it out before I told the other girls. I've been looking for y'all."

"Where did you see Chaim?"

"He came to find me. He works with the stuntmen sometimes, as you know, and one of them told him about the scene coming up and that it looked like they needed some women in it. So I thought I'd find out before I got everybody's hopes up."

"Well, good for Chaim. Where is he?"

"I don't know. He found me, told me, then ran off again."

"I love the way we take care of each other," I said with a broad smile. "But listen, Sandra. It's a go. No speculation. Freddy, that Greek assistant director guy, is the one who told me to find some of the girls. At least ten of you. So go back and get whatever girls you know that haven't already gone to the truck. Meet me at those trucks. They're near wardrobe, anyway. I'm sure there will be costumes for everyone."

"Okay, okay, Wilson, I'll meet you there after I get the others."

A scene with Sandra, I thought to myself as I walked back toward the trucks. I felt gleeful thinking about it.

"Wilson," someone called out as I arrived back at the trucks.

It was Chaim.

"They want us to board soon," he said in a serious tone. "We have to go to wardrobe first. Civilian attire this time. That's nice for a change. We have to dress here and leave our Marine gear at wardrobe, but in a pile for us to pick up later. I am just telling you what I heard."

Seeing old pictures of my parents always charmed me, but I felt ridiculous in my late-1940s suit when we returned to the set. The women in our group looked even more absurd in their loose-fitting dresses with ruffled sleeves and shoulders. Fedoras looked good on the men, I decided, once adapted to the suits we had on, but the broad-brimmed hats for the women were a joke. Such were the times.

"Walk casually down the streets," one of the assistant directors instructed us through his megaphone. "Talk occasionally, but do not exaggerate. We will not pick up what you are saying, but we need the visualization. We need a believable visualization, so act normally, please."

"You are walking too quickly," another of the assistant directors said to our group. "Relax, enjoy the sun and the conversation. Life is good."

"Soon you will hear a loud explosion," the first assistant director bellowed. "This will make you frantic. Do not exaggerate, but we do need you to yell out in fear and begin to run for shelter. There will be a building just in front of you when the explosion occurs. Everyone must run toward it. Do not trample one another or push your way into the building. It's all right to be crammed, but do *not* injure one another."

The explosion was accompanied by three small airplanes swooping down from behind us. The directors called out orders while we made our frantic efforts toward safety.

All in a day's work.

"It's a living," I said out loud on the bus taking us back to the base after we finished filming. "Everyone has to make a living, but I don't know if I want to do much of this. I suppose if I were rich and famous maybe it would be worth it. But I don't know if it's worth pursuing. Almost nobody makes it big in Hollywood."

"Thousands come to Hollywood with big dreams," Chaim added, "but the percentage that accomplish anything, and I don't mean stardom, is miniscule."

"If you have this big dream of acting, or being a movie star, then go for it," I continued. "But otherwise forget it."

"So what do you want to do with your life, Wilson?" Sunshine asked me loudly enough for everyone to hear.

"I don't know. Probably teach history."

"Teach history?" the Brit asked. "That is what interests you?"

"I love history," I explained. "I'll have a Master's degree soon and will teach high school with it. That's not so much money, but I would at least get by and love the subject. But I may go on for a doctorate and be a professor. Coming here and living history through the movie makes that very appealing, actually. But either way, I'll get by, and I love history."

"Well, you are doing pretty well for yourself just walking onto a set and being used with the real actors so much," Sunshine praised. "Movies may be worth it for you to pursue."

"Makes me wish I cared," I said with a sigh. "It's wasted on me. Except, I'm here. It makes it fun. For now. It just doesn't seem like worth the effort to me to take it seriously. If I knew I would make it, then I would pursue. But it seems like a waste to me, with the odds so slim and being bored with movie sets most of the time. I don't really enjoy this except for the novelty for now. Being rich and famous would make it worth it, but that's too long a shot."

"Listen to this man," the Frenchman said with a laugh. "It's wasted on him, he said. Then give it to me, *monsieur*. I would love to be an actor. Maybe not actor so much, but a movie star. Maybe I will try to find another movie after this."

"There is another movie going on," Sandra interrupted. "I heard there was, from one of the bit actors on the set. He's going to audition."

"Tell me about it if you hear more," the Frenchman requested.

"Sure," Sandra offered. "If I see him again, I'll ask him."

She looked back at me in a serious way, then turned away.

"I'm going to audition for that other movie," Sandra told me later that night in our room. "I didn't tell our friend that because I want it to be just you and me. I don't want him interfering with our adventure on this. So I told him my lie. Thank you for not spilling the beans. He can find things out on his own. But I would like to be in another movie, and with you."

"How are we going to be in two movies?" I quizzed her.

"We can't be, I know. But come with me to check the other one out. They are only forming now. Taking auditions, checking out sets. We could start on it when this one finishes. I hear we finish soon with the one we're doing now."

"Another Korean movie?" I mused aloud. "How many people care about this?"

"The director of this new one did one of the Tarzan movies before. I don't know which one. And there are so many. I don't know anything about the new movie except one is being prepared. It's cheaper to make movies here, so many independent movie makers are coming here. Sort of like Hong Kong. A lot of aspiring actors and directors go to Hong Kong to make movies now. Hong Kong makes so many Chinese Kung-Fu-type movies that now the British and Americans are going there because the movie set up is expanding but much cheaper. Same here. At least some. I guess some of the overflow is spilling over here."

"You are more interested in all this than I am," I

moaned. "I don't really have another movie in me.".

"The odds are against us anyway," she countered. "Just be with me. Let's at least try. We'd be extras again, but with luck maybe we could get bit parts in scenes. You know, with our experience here. And Freddy may be one of the assistants. That's in our favor."

I let out a laugh.

"So help me, Sandra. If we become movie stars now, I'll never forgive you."

"It's a deal," she said as she gave me a small kiss on the cheek. "If we become movie stars, I won't ever forgive you back."

Chapter 16

"Wilson," one of the stuntmen said as he walked up to me, "We're going to need you for a night scene. You'll need to be one of us again. We asked for you. You know us and take good direction. Roy Holland can do without you today as a stand-in. You'll be Army this time, though."

"I'll have to get Army gear again then, from wardrobe," I explained.

"We know that. We've already informed them. Leave your Marine gear there to be stored for you. You'll need it again tomorrow."

I almost brought up the incompetence of the girl in wardrobe, but hesitated. I was still angry with her for blowing my chance for a closeup scene. The stuntman sensed my concern.

"Your gear will be okay," he assured. "Someone will check on it after we leave here."

I grinned and nodded my head approvingly.

"We're going in a van," he continued. "There's just a few of us. It will be at night at an Army training area. Real soldiers doing real training, and they're going to let us do a scene in the movie for effect. Night fire with tracer rounds. Crossfire, even. It's part of their infantry training, and they're letting us observe. Night fire is very effective, so the producers and directors wanted to take advantage of it, and the Army went along. This will be a visual. In combat there's seldom tracer rounds. But we want to show the impact of hundreds of riflemen firing at the enemy. There won't really be an enemy out there where we're firing. One of MacArthur's men in the scene will explain why they are using tracer rounds for this battle. To intimidate green Commie troops or something. I'm not sure. Anyway, there will be a few closeup shots of us, the stuntmen, but we need more than just the Hollywood guys, so you came to mind as one to help pad the numbers for us. You'll be in a closeup."

I grinned his way. I missed the stuntmen.

"And we could use Chaim too, the Israeli, if you see him. I was going to tell him this too."

I looked over at Sandra, who was among the extras nearby waiting around to be used.

"Can she come with us?" I asked.

He looked at me and grimaced. He kept his intense stare while he thought.

"Bring her along," he said. "We may need a nurse in the scene, you never know. Or a frantic missionary. We'll see."

I rushed over to Sandra.

"They're using me for a scene tonight near some US Army base," I told her. "And they said I could bring you just in case they need a girl extra for some reason."

"Why would they need just one girl?" Sunshine asked interrupting.

She then put on an exaggerated grin to add to the mischief. I pondered what she said.

"Yeah, you too, Sunshine," I replied with authority. "Worth a try."

"Ahhhh!" Sunshine howled. "Yes! Yes!"

"But when we show up to get in the van this afternoon," I instructed, "act like you know what you are doing. As a matter of fact, Chaim is going with us too. Sunshine, you walk with him to the van when we board, and then sit next to him on the way."

None of the stuntmen mentioned either girl as we all walked to the van we were to board later that afternoon. The stuntman in charge studied both Sandra and Sunshine curiously, then went about his business. Sunshine realized our stowaway scheme was working and smiled.

I had seen much of the Korean countryside by now. I barely noticed it this time as we rode along, since my mind was preoccupied with the upcoming movie shot. Could the girls somehow be slipped into all this, I pondered? Combat scene or not, was there some setting where my two women companions fit into all the goings-on?

Our van eventually travelled on small, bumpy dirt roads to an open meadow. Just in front of us were several hundred soldiers in their helmets and fatigues, being dispersed and spread out in a large row through the width of the training field around us. Farther on in front of us were small hills. The soldiers, so we were told by Freddy, would be firing into these hills. Some would be firing at a slight angle to the left, while others at a slight angle to the right. The result of the glowing tracer bullets crossing each other before hitting the hills for targets would be a piercing display of illuminated firepower brought out in full force by the surrounding darkness.

"Stuntmen, be on the ready," Freddy cautioned.

"Wilson," the stuntman that recruited me for the

scene called out, "you and Chaim come with us. Put on your helmet. We'll give you rifles when we get to our set. These soldiers here in training will be firing M16s. That's the modern combat rifle these days. We'll be using M1s, however, the weapon of the times. The close-ups will be of us supposedly firing the correct rifles. Ours will contain blanks, however. It will be just for show, and you'll have to give them back as soon as we are finished filming. All this trouble for just one scene, to give this battle a personal touch, so to speak— a squad of soldiers maneuvering while the real soldiers make a fireworks display with their tracer rounds in the dark. I hope this makes some sense to you."

I rushed quickly to Sandra and Sunshine, who were standing near the van that brought us.

"There's nothing for you in this," I said, "so you'll have to stay far enough away from us, but near enough so you can be used just in case they need women for something. We're adlibbing all this about you right now. No one but me knows what you're doing here. Sort of. So, stay several yards away, but in our vicinity. It will be dark. Hopefully, no one will be paying attention."

Those of us in the stuntman crew walked over to a corner of the field where lighting equipment and cameras stood. There were boxes of costumes and equipment in a truck to the side.

"Quiet on the set," Freddy bellowed. "Quiet on the set. Please await instruction from our director."

Director Jillette sat impatiently in his folding chair and stared at the soldiers in front of him—in particular, at the small group of us who were to be the center of action. He then caught a glimpse of Sandra and

Sunshine just behind one of the trucks with equipment.

"Wait, wait," he said with a sneer. "Who are these girls? Who brought these girls with us just now? There are no parts for women in any of this. This is for night fire and our squad of soldiers here darting from one part of the action to another. Nothing else. No spectators here. Someone could get hurt and hold up everything. Get these women out of here. Who brought them?"

"I did, sir," I said nervously.

"You did?" Director Jillette asked with a pronounced sneer. "And who the hell are you that brought them? Tell me now. Just who the hell are you? Aren't you this character we've been using a lot lately? So you are the director now, since you think you are some big shot that got to be in a Hollywood movie?"

"I told them to come along," said the stuntman that recruited Chaim and myself. "Just as a precaution, Mr. Jillette. It's nighttime in a remote area, and I heard that perhaps some Korean civilians might be a good background with maybe some women. To play a role like stranded refugee types from a village. Just to be safe, sir, we asked them to come along. Just in case you needed to make a setting. If not, then we don't use them. But I didn't want to have to find someone at this time and place if we needed them."

Director Jillette thought for a moment.

"Damn good," he said with a laugh. "That is damn good. Right you are. Damn right you are. I love entrepreneurs. You are going to go far. That is perfect. A couple of American white women, just in case, for a frantically desperate scene of some sort. Right. Right. Yes. I'll hold on to that thought. We just may use a couple of frantic white women for something like that.

It's dark. We don't have to put them as the center of attention. Just enough light to see they are scared refugee types scurrying somewhere for cover."

He then turned toward the girls.

"Go with this director here, the one handling our special soldiers for this scene, and get into some early-fifties dresses and get ready to scurry about like scared Chicken Littles. If we didn't bring dresses in that truck, put on pants. Doesn't matter. Is that agreeable to you two?"

"Yes, sir," Sandra and Sunshine said in unison.

"In the meantime," Director Jillette yelled out into his megaphone to heighten the mood, "we're going to get the scene set up. So hurry along now. Be back in half an hour. Follow your assistant director friend. He'll fix you up."

I smirked broadly enough I was sure everyone could see. *Make your own luck, indeed*, I gloated inside.

We waited past twilight until things were pitch dark. The illuminated crossfire would show up, but there needed to be enough lighting to detect shadowy soldier figures firing the rifles. Not so much light, however, as to distinguish the use of M16s instead of M1s. Hollywood specialists in such lighting had to get it just right to produce the correct effect.

Nearby, the stuntmen prepared for the combat scene. It had to be coordinated with the live fire close by since we needed the sound effects of the soldiers firing their rifles. The lighting for this combat had to be bright enough to detect soldiers maneuvering in the darkness with M1s and occasionally firing at a supposed enemy.

"Drop," Freddy barked out. "Drop now," he

repeated to the stuntmen of which I was a part. "The enemy is ahead, and they are shooting at you. Fire at them. Keep firing. We can see the flash of your rifles with the blanks. That is good."

We simulated battle for a few seconds and then were ordered to get up again to charge a few feet farther into the darkness, then ordered to drop and fire again.

"You are hit," an assistant director yelled to one of the stuntmen. "The one designated to be shot is now hit. Fall to earth. Very good."

The victim jerked on cue while supposedly dying.

"All but the hit victim, get up," the assistant director shouted further. "One more charge until I say fall again. Charge, yes, charge. Good, now drop to the ground."

"Very good," Director Jillette praised while observing the scene. "Very good. This was effective. We will coordinate the scenes with the editing in Rome later, after we leave here. But we have what we need to work with."

He then looked at the assistant director for more instruction.

"Okay, we lost one of our soldiers. Our comrade. So take your group of stuntmen actors and settle this portion of the scene like we discussed earlier today. We now have to stumble back to find his body and identify who bought the farm. We'll have just enough lighting to see some somber faces. We lost our comrade. All you stuntmen have to feel the pain and show the pain. Quiet, solemn pain. Then the small eulogy before heading back to camp with the body. A small drama of losing a lost comrade and then the scene is over for the night."

The open field where we performed as a squad of combat soldiers was lit well enough that we could see where we were going. Three times we ran, then fell to earth to fire, then up again. In one of the running segments, a professional stuntman was "mortally wounded" for effect. Chaim and I were on the edge of this squad so we could be cut if we did not perform well.

"Don't overact, Chaim," I coached him as we circled the body of the fallen soldier. "Just look sad, but not dramatic."

"Ha," he returned. "My acting coach. Thanks. But you are right. I have lost friends to war. I know well how I felt when I bid them goodbye as I watched them be buried."

I wore a pained, blank stare as the camera focused on me before moving to the others. I didn't know if anyone watching the movie would recognize me, but I would know who I was in this scene. I was determined not to be cut out because I wasn't looking the part.

"Anyone want to say anything for eulogy?" a colleague of the victim asked in the scene.

"When the roll is called up yonder, I'll be there," another of the stuntmen said for effect. "Until then, buddy, you'll be in our hearts."

Another of the stuntmen began to sing a sad song I'd never heard before. He sang it stiffly and in near monotone.

"Wait a minute," the assistant director in charge of us moaned. "This isn't going to work. Was this supposed to be one of the grunts singing a dirge or some lonely song? I don't even know this song, and no one else will either. We need better. And a better singer. How did this happen with this song now? Someone else. Anyone. Quickly, audition quickly. Sing a couple of lines of 'America the Beautiful' or something. Let me hear what you sound like."

"Wilson can sing," Chaim said before anyone sang their audition.

"Wilson? Wilson can sing? Let me hear you, Wilson."

"I even know a Texas dirge," I said.

"Go then," the assistant director said impatiently. "We haven't time for this. We must all go back soon."

I sang a cowboy dirge common back home. As if for this moment.

"I know this song," one of the stuntmen said after I finished two lines of it. "That's 'The Streets of Laredo,' isn't it? I used to sing it as a kid back in Oklahoma."

"Yes," I concurred. "A cowboy's dirge. It's beautiful. It's not a kid's song. It's a beautiful dirge to a fallen comrade."

Chaim looked at me in admiration. I remembered our night back at the hostel when I sang for the first time. As if this scene was ordained to happen now.

"Perfect," the assistant director praised. "Perfect. And you sing it well. Good. Good. We don't have to find Frank Sinatra or someone and pay them. We'll double your salary for the night though, Wilson. And you can tell your grandchildren that's you in this movie and then sing to them to prove it. You're richer, we're richer, and Director Jillette won't fire us for this scene."

Chapter 17

"Are you the one they call Superman?" a slim, young Korean girl asked me.

Her hair was long, black, and combed back, leaving her face displayed prominently. I looked up at her from the table where I sat in the commons area of the hostel.

"Yes," I answered her.

"I am embarrassed to be here," she told me. "I know Americans stay here. Sometimes I want to talk to an American. I do not like so much the military Americans, however. And people think bad things about you if you are seen with an American soldier."

"I understand," I said. "Most are very good guys, but some do have a bad reputation. I understand your concern."

"It embarrasses me to be here at this hostel also," she emphasized. "I said that already, I know. I am nervous. People talk about the girls that look for Americans. But I am a student at the university. People talk bad also about Americans at these hostels, not just bad soldiers. Hippies are here, I am told. I am sorry. I do not mean to insult you. You have short hair and no beard. I think you are not a hippie. My curiosity brings me here. I did not come to insult. I am so feeling awkward. My apology."

"I understand. It's okay. Thanks for talking to me.

Yes, there are all kinds of people at hostels. But most of these people are also good. Just like the soldiers. I understand the concerns, however. It's okay. I'm not insulted."

"Thank you for your understanding."

She studied me, still showing awkwardness.

"Do you mind if we talk a bit?" she asked shyly. "I study American civilization and also English. I hope to be a professor someday. So do you mind if we talk? I would like to get to know you. Please, sir."

I glanced over at Sandra, who sat across from me, to see what she thought. She gave a quick nod of approval.

"I'd love to talk to you," I told her.

"Yes, thank you. You are indeed nice. Sometimes Korean friends come here to enjoy all the Americans. How you sing with the guitars here and talk about America and Europe. These places that interest me. And about your studies you do at your universities back home. I am too embarrassed to come here until now. But my friends that sometime visit here told me about this one they call Superman. Such a funny name, but they say you are very nice and have many adventures. So I would like to know you if that is pleasant for you."

I glanced again at Sandra, who reassured me.

"Of course," I said with a smile. "That is very nice of you. You can sit at this table. Or we can go somewhere. What would you like?"

"Please, let us go somewhere. But not tonight. I would look like a prostitute. Could we meet tomorrow and go somewhere? Tomorrow is Sunday. You are free, I think, and I have no school. I could show you a park nearby, and we have a nice restaurant available. It serves only hamburgers. That is not so nice or fancy, but upstairs they have a music room I would like to share with you. They play classical music. You know, Mozart and Beethoven. You would enjoy. We could have a coffee or even a wine. Is this all right with you, Mr. Superman."

"Call me Wilson. Wilson is my real name. Superman is just a nickname I got here."

"Yes, I wondered something about this name. Such a strange name. So, Wilson, I could come by here tomorrow to get you. To meet you at this table is fine. Nine o'clock, perhaps. Is that pleasant with you? I hoped you were this Superman person. Tall, pleasant looks, blue eyes, and brown hair. Not so many look this appearance, so I thought you are this person I have heard about."

"Sure, thank you for the compliments. And nine o'clock is good for me. Thanks. I am looking forward to it."

She held out her hand to shake mine.

"Yes, you are indeed such a nice person. Just like I heard. I will not be so embarrassed if I am with you, I think. I do not want to lose face among my countrymen."

"Thank you," I replied, oozing in sympathy for her. "What is your name?"

"My American name for me, for the university class, is Maria. You know, like the virgin of the God Jesus. I am Christian, by the way. So I chose Maria to be my American name."

"Sure, Maria. I'll see you tomorrow. I am looking forward to it."

"Thank you. I will be here. Nine o'clock. In this

outside area with the tables for recreation enjoyment with friends. Thank you again."

Sandra and I watched her walk away.

"I guess she didn't catch I was with you," I said apologetically to Sandra.

"That is so sweet, Wilson. She was so nervous. It took courage for her to come here. She wanted to talk to someone, to you, so badly. Please go with her, Wilson. I won't be jealous. I admire her, actually. So please go with her tomorrow. That's what we're here for, even. You and me, I mean. Sort of. Not just for history, but culture."

Later that night, as Sandra and I lay together in our darkened room, I tried to picture what she might really think. She had to have some reservations somewhere about my endeavor tomorrow. She trusted me, and I intended to live up to that trust. Vowing that to myself helped me drift off to sleep.

That is, until Sandra turned toward me, waking me up, later on.

"Wait a minute, Wilson," Sandra said forcefully.

"Wait, what?" I asked nervously as I twisted toward her.

"She said she was taking you to a hamburger joint that played Beethoven. I want to go. I gotta see this."

"You disturbed me to tell me that?" I asked with a playful bite. "Why aren't you asleep, Sandra? My God. Have you slept at all? You're making me regret I'm going with her."

"Good," Sandra teased. "Good. You need to have some regret somewhere in you. But no, I want you to go. But as I'm trying to sleep I envision you drinking wine to Beethoven while eating hamburgers. That's got to be a show. And I admit, just a little too cozy."

"Yeah," I said with a chuckle as I pictured it. "A good memory ready to happen. Later we'll go. You and me. I'll get the address. Maybe they have a business card. Anyway, we'll go on our own. Even if it sucks and I hate it. Just to say we did something like this in Korea in our good old days."

"Our good old days?" Sandra mused out loud. "Yours and mine, you mean. Like as if we're going to know each other later on in Texas after Korea now?"

"What do you think? This ain't no fling between us. Even if we move along in our lives after Korea, we're going to want to relive the good old days. I've told you my feelings for you. Even that I love you."

"Yes, I know. I love you too, Wilson, so it makes sense. I guess I don't want to think about 'after Korea.' I'm just living the day-by-day in spite of feelings. I don't know what to expect about anything after Korea. But now you've got me nervous. There is going to be an 'after Korea' someday, I know. For us, I mean. I don't want to think about all that. I'm having too much fun."

"I like thinking about it," I answered. "And about a relationship with you. I can live day to day and still like the thought of you in my life. So relax, Sandra. We're both from Texas, and we're both working on our thesis. It's going to be nice going back, and you know to hell we're going to see each other."

She touched my neck gently with her fingertips.

"That's reassuring," she said. "Good. Good. Yes, reassure me. You enjoy your hamburger and Beethoven with Maria then. I'm fine here until we go ourselves later on. And I like the thought of seeing you after we leave here and go back to school. I knew we would see each other later. It's common sense. But I like the reassurance. We're half way around the world and having a great time together, with feelings I adore. But I don't want to make all these plans when we are students in two different universities and all. Something will work out. Right now, I don't know what."

"I can sleep now?" I asked. "We'll enjoy all this and know things will work out, right?"

Sandra laid her head on my shoulder with her hand on my chest. She began to drum her fingertips as she did so. I melted.

I got up early the next morning. I tried reading as I waited in the commons area but had a difficult time concentrating. Soon, I caught a glimpse of Maria as she entered. She held a serious, stiff demeanor as she walked toward me. She seemed unsure of herself.

"Hello," I greeted her as she stood before me.

"Hello, Wilson. Have you eaten breakfast?"

"Have you?" I asked to be courteous so she could decide if she wanted to share a meal with me or not.

"I ate an egg," she replied. "It will keep me until we have our hamburger."

"I had an egg too," I said. "I love the eggs this vendor out in front makes. Hard boiled but in a special sauce. I'm addicted to them, I think."

"Shall we go then?" she asked straightforwardly.

We walked out onto the sidewalk in front of the hostel.

"I have a car," she informed. "It will save us time and trouble."

Did Maria have money, then? A student, but with a car?

"Watch your legs," she said apologetically as I readied to enter her small vehicle. "This car is a miniature. But you will fit."

It was quite a squeeze for me to get into, even after I pushed back the seat.

"Pusan is an enormous town," she said as she drove us, still so businesslike. "We will not see many places today. Have you seen much of Pusan?"

"Only from the bus, and usually at night. Sometimes I don't know when to get off, and we drive past the hostel here. You would think I would know my way by now, but at night I don't recognize all the landmarks. So I've seen more of Pusan than I should have for my circumstances."

"Why did you come to Korea, Wilson? Why would an American, not a soldier, come to our country? I would never leave America."

"I am a student, like you. At a university in Texas, where I grew up. Writing a thesis about the war here back in the fifties. I wanted to do research, and I prefer doing some of that research here, to make it more personal."

"So much trouble to do that. And expensive. Americans have so much money."

"I suppose, compared to here. But I don't have that much. I borrow to go to school. Now this. I will have to pay it off someday."

"You have so much confidence you can have such a job. I suppose I will get a job also, with my college education. That is not a guarantee. But probably. But I like education, even if I do not get a job."

"Me too," I concurred. "I love education. Books. Traveling."

"We are approaching a park, Wilson. I want to walk quietly with you. Share with you the quiet of this area of the city."

I had no idea where we were.

"Why did you choose to write your thesis about our war here, Wilson?" she asked as we walked around.

"The war was what I first heard about the world when I was little," I answered. "Before school age, when it was being fought. Many of my relatives were over here during the war then. I wanted to share those memories now in my adulthood."

"We struggle here, Wilson. And to see someone that has everything and could be anywhere, but comes here—I wonder why this is so."

I shrugged at the idea of her analysis.

"You are my first American. The first I have gotten to know. Even this much to know. You said you are from Texas."

"Did I tell you that? Oh, yeah, I told you I grew up there."

"I knew it from when I found out about you before, from my friends that visit your hostel sometimes."

"What do you know about Texas?" I asked.

"You killed Kennedy," she responded.

I let out a loud laugh.

"Wow," I huffed. "I was expecting something about cowboys or going to the moon or something. But wow. I killed Kennedy."

"That was tragic," she sighed as she glanced at me for emphasis. "That was terrible, Wilson. Why was he hated so by people in Texas? We loved him in Korea. He was a great statesman."

"He wasn't hated," I answered defensively. "He

was by some, I guess. Everyone is hated by someone. He was a new, modern President in a new age. Some liked him for that. Others felt threatened by change."

"He had vision," she said with respect. "He gave so many people hope. And he was so young. So much promise. Evil must destroy all hope. Why this?"

"Thank you for liking President Kennedy," I said sympathetically. "It touches me when people want this hope he offered. Or stood for."

"The war here destroyed so many lives," she said sharply. "There is so much evil. Kim, the dictator of North Korea, is so evil. We hate our own despots. Syngman Rhee, now Park. But Kim in North Korea is so evil. Like Stalin and like Mao in one man. It is so frightening. He is Korean and rules so much like a tyrant. And right here in the northern half of our peninsula. Only America saves us. How does such evil win? Until the war we hated the Americans. America kept Syngman Rhee as our ruler. But after the North conquered us and brutalized us, we could only wish for something better."

"We didn't give you Syngman Rhee," I corrected her. "We hate these dictators like him. We didn't come to conquer you. But the Communists are even worse. We are trying to stop the spread of Nazi-like evil. That's the Communists. They are like the Nazis. We would have to take over and rule you to keep a Syngman Rhee from gaining power. We choose to hold the Communists at bay and work with the local despots and hopefully minimize their damage. That's the best we know to do for now."

"No one believes that, Wilson. Everyone believes you controlled him and approved his horrors. The world is so cruel. But after you helped us drive out the Communists, we were willing to accept anything better."

"I know how things look," I said with frustration. "But that is my point. Syngman Rhee was at least better than the alternative presented by the Communists. And maybe we have the military and economic might to conquer all these countries in the rest of the third world in the name of joy and happiness, but no one wants to conquer anyone. We get blamed for it, but we don't do it. We got blamed over Vietnam. We tried freeing that country from the threat of Communism there, and everyone blamed us for that. So we work with the lesser of evils when we can and try to work for better things. I know it doesn't look like it or make sense."

"I didn't bring you to this park to torture you with guilt. I appreciate the Americans. Things are so much better now because you are here. And we are getting a better economy and education, too. So I am grateful to America. And I now have an American friend. This makes me happy."

I nodded approval.

"No more politics, Wilson. It was good to talk about our circumstances, but let's enjoy the rest of our time now."

"That's a good idea, Maria, but can you introduce me someday to some of your professors that can help my research about the war? That was my big hope in coming to Korea in the first place. That and just getting a feel for the place where all this happened."

"Yes, Wilson. Yes, I would like that. Thank you for not just coming here to read a book and pretend you know something. Yes, this makes me happy to find good professors for your research. I will do this for you."

Maria seemed pacified as we walked to her restaurant of choice. I was glad she seemed pleased with me and that I had finally befriended a Korean.

She led me to a wooden structure near the park that was two stories high. I was charmed by this restaurant immediately. The room on the bottom floor where we ate was little bigger than an average living room back home. Ten tables with chairs were squeezed inside, leaving barely enough room to have a place to sit. Almost all of the tables were taken by customers.

"These are students," Maria explained. "The university begins just across the street here. This restaurant is a favorite place for some of us. I live in a bed-and-breakfast room nearby."

"This restaurant looks like a hamburger joint might look back home," I replied.

"Yes, it has an American atmosphere. That appeals to some people."

"Does it you?" I asked.

"I approve, yes. I like Americans. Not always the soldier. Some of them want a female for comfort, and I am uneasy around this type. But I like Americans, and that is why I decided I wanted to meet an American man that I might like better than a soldier."

I grinned approval.

"Tell me more why you write this thesis about our war here in the fifties. I think I chose the right American to get to know."

I thought how to answer.

"Somehow this little peninsula here became a world focal point during the war," I began. "This peninsula where I am now has been here for millennia, but from out of nowhere it became important suddenly. Either to further the cause of world justice through enforced socialism by a great leader like Kim in the North, or to further world imperialism by American slave masters."

"You are being a joker now," she said with a laugh. "This is called sarcasm, I think."

"Sarcasm," I agreed.

"But seriously, Wilson, why does America care about us? I am glad you do. I am glad you are here, like I said, but I do not understand why. Perhaps that is why people think you are imperialists. Why else would you be here?"

"It's not for the kimchee."

"You are not here for the kimchee, you say? Oh, I should hope you are here for this. Then we could also be imperialists. First we conquer you with our food, then our culture. But really, Wilson, why does America care about us?"

"America used to be a colony," I explained. "It made us pity the underdog. You know the little guy that gets pushed around by the bully. And once we got our freedom, we proclaimed the Monroe Doctrine. This doctrine stands up to European imperialistic powers in our entire hemisphere. It's in our cultural makeup to pull for the underdog."

"But we are not in your hemisphere. This is half way around the world."

"We still had cultural ties with Europe when the Nazis tried to take over there. So we already had awareness of a bigger world than ourselves. And fighting Japan during World War II after they bombed us in Hawaii made us aware of this part of the world. And now there are jet airplanes around. Any place in the world is not so far away from us.

"Then the Communists started taking over countries. It just seemed personal to us after a while to see all these bullies around, especially remembering World War II, and with our pity for the underdog when there's the threat that one power could enslave so much of the world. There was colonialism when there were just ships, but now with airplanes and tanks and cars, it is easy to feel threatened from anywhere. World War I was so brutal. We hoped to never have another war. But then came the Nazis, then Stalin. Not fighting did not bring peace. So here we are. The world superpower. It matters if we as a superpower fight or don't fight."

"I am so glad you are here," she said yet again. "Russia started the Korean War, then China got involved. Here we are, the hermit kingdom not allowed to be left alone. And our saviors come from half way around the world. And now you and I have coffee together. Well, a soda drink, perhaps, and a hamburger."

"I am glad we are here too," I said. "And also glad I am here with you now. I hate war, but here it is anyway in our lives. There is Cuba, a little island so close to us that we feel threatened by it. There are colonies in Africa still from the European days, but now there are Russian puppets there too. Nothing is going away. But while all this happens, yes, here we are talking about it and studying about it at my university and yours. So there is more good than bad, I think."

She smiled. This charmed me.

"Listen, do you hear this song on the speakers

now?" she asked. "This masterpiece that is playing now? Yes, this small world we all share happily. So let us share Vivaldi together also. Music from Europe but enjoyed by Americans and also by us in Korea. *The Four Seasons* this music piece is called. Oh, I think the most wonderful arrangement of music ever. It is so thrilling to hear. Quick, finish eating. No, take your time so we can enjoy this glory of music now. But soon we must go upstairs. There is a room, and it has only benches to sit. You will see. We must go there. And bring our wine. It is music for wine that they play here."

I found myself adoring Maria. I could not remember being so charmed with anyone like I was now with her. I loved that I was in Korea just to savor the moments I spent with her. We finished our meal quietly while we listened to the classical masterpieces played over the speakers.

There was a large chalkboard in the room upstairs where Maria took me afterward. The room was crowded, and I was the only white person there. The rest were Asian, probably Korean. I felt like a hick around them. They were unassuming as they listened. They seemed to fit in the restaurant downstairs, eating their hamburgers, but also now while appreciating the classics they were sharing. Their appreciation appeared genuine.

"Look," Maria said, pointing at the words printed in large bold letters in the center of the chalkboard. "That is what is playing now. Brahms Symphony Number Four in E Minor. Oh, Wilson, it is so moving. This student you see sitting at the chalkboard, he erases the previous song and then writes what is playing now.

It is clumsy to do this, writing in chalk, but it is devoted. I love this devotion. I love this music. I love being here with you."

I was more moved than at any time in my life. I was sure of it. I began to think of Sandra now, to discipline myself. I was afraid of falling for Maria.

"Thank you, Wilson," Maria said as we left the room to go back downstairs and outside. "My one time with an American was better than I ever dreamed. I will remember this every time I see a soldier look at me for comfort fantasies about me. This means much to me to have been together with you today. I do not want to know only of such Americans as some of these soldiers. It has been a wonderful day."

"This will be a cherished memory for me, Maria. Thank you so much for inviting me."

"Wilson," she said in a serious tone. "I must never feel affection for an American. I don't want to say romantic affection. But maybe that is the word. I could never explain to my family any pleasure about an American man. But I am so glad I invited you. I will marry a Korean man someday, and we will have good children, but I will know there are such as you in America.

"This was special for me. In America I think you say 'liberated.' I feel liberated from knowing you, Wilson. 'Liberated' is a better word than 'romantic,' I think. And I know, from my friends that saw you at the hostel before, that you have an American girlfriend there. That makes me happy so that we do not feel romantic for each other. It is wonderful to be friends. Only friends. Then to live our lives in our countries."

She held out her hand to shake mine. It was

mundane to do so, an anticlimax, but it was another experience worth living during my time in Korea.

Chapter 18

"Hello, Sarge," I said with a smile.

The middle-aged potbellied Army staff sergeant gave me a quick, indifferent glance, then kept walking on toward the large group of extras behind me. His usual entourage of Army NCOs followed him, some scoping me out as they walked past me.

"He doesn't like you for some reason," Sandra said, bemused. "Did you say something wrong?"

I shook my head no while displaying my frustration with his attitude.

"I wonder if he thinks I'm a hippie," I said with a bite.

"You have short hair, new clean clothes, and you don't wear any peace medallions. You're courteous to people. Respectful. That's not hippie."

"I don't know what these lifers think," I replied. "That's what they call them. Lifers. Career military. The enlisted men that want out as soon as their enlistment is up call them that. It's meant to be disrespectful. All the more reason I wanted to show respect. I don't like hippies, peaceniks, or enlisted soldiers that hate their jobs in the service. I'm from Texas. More than that, I was in the Corps at Texas A&M and will get a commission when I finish my Master's degree. I want to show appreciation and respect to these guys who are serving and getting little respect for it. But I'm getting sick of these guys myself. The lifer types. I guess to them all backpackers look alike."

"I'm glad you're getting a commission," Sandra said. "We need more like you. But hang in there. You'll have more than fighting Commies to handle when you go in. The military itself is having problems these days. Morale, self-respect. Ever since Vietnam. It hasn't really recovered from years of an unpopular war."

"Quite a challenge." I pondered about it. "And every one of these guys I'm showing respect to have two-inch foreheads and forty-inch waist lines. God, I hope we don't get into a war anytime soon."

"Superman?" the new girl in our hostel group, the one from L.A., came in. "I'm a leftover from the sixties. I'm not into the military. But I've mellowed a bit since the antiwar demonstration times. Knocking the military was old-hat, back in the day. I never really knew anyone in the military, though. They were just this commodity of the era. An ornament of the establishment to knock. But I agree with you. It's getting scary now, seeing these guys up close like we are. Not so much because you just got snubbed. I'm sort of used to that mindset, in the cultural wars and all. But it's scary to think that this military in front of us is what stands between us and Russia or China. Suddenly, it matters to me. I'm in the part of the world smack dab between Russia and China. So it's personal now. I feel myself wanting a strong, and sane, military. But what I'm seeing is what I really hoped was some stereotype my crowd invented. I'm scared those stereotypes are true. All the things I wanted to be down on, you know. Somehow they really exist after all, and I wish I wasn't seeing it."

I thought what to say to add to the mood among us. Feeling myself agree with my cultural counterpart confused me. Is this how it begins, I wondered, to see more of the other side and feeling conflict inside from it? But I knew I was not from their world, the counter-culture one. Yet my new environment as an outsider with the Army sergeant presented opportunity for some perspective. Don't join the either-or world, I told myself. It's not conservative versus liberal that matters, but broadened perspectives.

"It's hard not to be judgmental," I replied to Sandra and the girl from L.A. "I still want to get commissioned. I still respect the military. But I'm not going to put up with any Neanderthal type. It makes me want to join the military all the more. To do something constructive about the situation."

I thought to say more, but decided to drop it.

"We need extras," Freddy called out. "Extras over here. Follow me. We are going to the hill in front of us now. Some of you will follow the cattle trail up it. The path, I mean. We call this a cattle trail back home. This worn footpath up this hill."

He looked at me.

"Wilson, you will lead the extras up this path. We will film part of this group as it climbs. Find your stunt crew extras amongst you. Form at the base of the hill until I tell you to climb."

He looked at the small remnant of extras at hand.

"Follow Wilson here to the base of the hill and wait on instructions," he emphasized.

The path to the hill was the length of a football field. I waited for further instruction when we arrived.

"Okay, Wilson," Freddy said. "Ascend the path. It is not far to the other side. Wait there."

"I'll take them," one of the pot-bellied soldiers yelled out. "I'll make it realistic. A real forced march. Those that can't keep up, don't bother to follow."

The soldier and his colleagues began the walk up the path, minus the pot-bellied career sergeant who had been leading them until now.

"You've got to be kidding me," I moaned to Chaim. "These dorks are just taking over. Can't they see what good shape you and I are in? Especially compared to the likes of them?"

"I'm going too," the L.A. girl said with a snicker. "My grandmother could keep up with these guys."

Sandra looked at me as she rolled her eyes while shaking her head.

"I'm ashamed to tell my father about these jokers," she groaned. "He's from the old days."

It was barely more than a stroll up the hill as we walked behind the pot-gutted self-appointed leader. No one among us broke into a sweat.

"You did good," the soldier leader praised us arrogantly. He seemed to feel accomplished.

"Board the trucks here," an assistant director waiting on us instructed. "We must go to the village just ahead. Stuntmen, form up when we arrive. You must rescue an orphanage in the scene there. There are Korean actors waiting on us for this, but we will use some of the women here also to be rescued."

"That's you, Sandra," I coaxed.

"I'm ready," she said. "I just hope it's you that saves me, though, and not these goons leading us. For my sanity."

The village for the scene was chosen because there were many buildings in it that were half destroyed. Perhaps, I thought, from the war itself, years before.

"Wilson," the lead stuntman called out as we prepared for a battle scene. "We're going to charge through that rubble on the other side of the street. There will be an explosion. Keep running through the smoke created from it. That is the main visual for this portion. Don't get wounded or limp or anything fancy for this. Play it straight. We're simply going to charge. When you reach the other side, I want you to run into one of the buildings. They'll edit what they need from this."

Some of the Army soldiers were placed just ahead of us. One of them lit a cigarette.

"He's hamming it up on purpose," I complained to my stuntman colleague. "And the directors are going to allow it. They are going to allow this corn. God!"

"Chill out, Wilson," the stuntman said with a laugh. "They'll probably edit the guy out. Just do your part. You'll be getting most of the attention in all of this, not them."

"I bet they don't edit out anything," I whined while showing my frustration as I walked.

"It's cool," the stuntman chided me further. "I mean it. Chill out. I'm glad you take it all seriously, but most of these scenes will get cut out. They're just letting the cameras roll. Anyway, it's all the better for us then. We make better soldiers."

"In more ways than one," I said in disgust.

Chapter 19

"Wilson," Freddy called out as he walked over to me, "it's quiet here for us this afternoon. I'm taking advantage of the lull in shooting to check out another movie being made nearby. There's a small independent movie to be made soon. It begins shortly after ours finishes."

"When will that be?" I asked him curiously. "The completion of our filming of this Pusan movie, I mean."

"We should be finished in a couple of weeks. They have filming and editing to do in Italy, but the Army and Marine action scenes here are near finishing."

"Italy?"

"Yes," Freddy answered. "Italy is a major producer of movies these days. There is no Italian connection in our movie, but in the film-making world you access the best facilities at the least cost."

"That's capitalism," I said with a grin.

"Yes, it is," he answered with a laugh. "Socialism in the Hollywood world is for cocktail parties and political rallies. Movie producers are among the most cutthroat capitalists anywhere. And that right there is why Hollywood thrives—from the accountability and opportunities of capitalism. The studios in Italy are often high quality and cheap. So some filming and editing will be done there that does not need all this military background. But back to why I came to talk to you."

He studied me a bit.

"You seem ambitious, Wilson. Perhaps you have a future in the movie world. I don't know if you've thought about it. But I'm on my way to see the director of a movie ready to be made. It's an hour's drive from here. They're preparing the setting for some scenes now. Filming will begin in a month. Now is the time to talk to them."

"About what?" I inquired.

"About being in it. I want to join them as an assistant director. I telephoned the director for this movie. I don't know him, but I worked with one of his assistant directors before. This is a chance for you to pursue another bit part, if you like. I can put in a good word for you."

"Really?" I asked. This astonished me. "Why would they be interested in me? I only had one small speaking role here."

"You have charisma. And looks. And now a bit of experience. While you are here, pursue this. See if you can get noticed again like you did with this movie now. You *will* be noticed if I can be an assistant for that movie. I can help you, I think."

"Can I bring Sandra?" I asked Freddy. "She is one of the extras. She's been here almost as long as I have. She already told me about the movie you just mentioned. I wasn't interested then. Sounds okay now."

"Yes, bring her. It's worth a try. I've seen her with you at times. Yes, she has presence. I have my car. We can take her."

"What about Chaim?" I asked, pushing things. "He's one of the stuntmen extras with me, the one that told me about our movie to begin with, way back. I feel I owe him."

Freddy laughed.

"Yes. We can only hope. Bring him."

"And Sunshine. She's a girl extra also. The blonde-haired girl who's well endowed. She's from Sweden, but her English is flawless. No accent."

"Buxomed Swedish blondes are also welcome, Wilson. But that is enough. The odds are against us, you must know. We can leave now, if your friends are available, but we must hurry. I know where to go. My friend there is waiting on me. On us, I should say. Go get your friends."

Luckily, my cohorts from the hostel were all together where I had left them before.

"Sandra," I called out as I approached them. "Sandra? Hey! Guess what?"

"You're excited, Wilson. Are they going to use you specially again for something? Did you get me a part too or something?"

"There is a movie ready to be shot after the one we're in now. I bet this is the movie you told me about before."

She nodded her head. "I'm sure," she replied.

"I stumbled onto a connection for this movie, and we need to check it out."

"Wow. It pays to be your girlfriend."

"Yes, it does. But don't get your hopes up yet."

"I know to never get my hopes up," she returned. "I show up and get my thirty-five bucks, and anything else is gravy."

"One of the assistant directors, the one named Freddy, has a car and wants a job with this new movie.

It begins filming right about the time this one ends. He said maybe in a couple of weeks or so. So you, me, Sunshine, and Chaim are invited to come along with him if you want."

Sandra looked at me, bewildered, as if nothing I said made sense.

"Why the four of us?" she asked. "Did you get the offer? I bet you did, and you got us involved with you."

She rubbed my cheek affectionately at the thought.

"Well," I said as a follow-through, "maybe. Anyway, we're leaving now, if you want to go. I'm going."

"Sure," she answered. "Just like that. Sure. Yeah. Let's go."

"Sunshine and Chaim too," I added.

"I heard my name," Sunshine said chirpily a few yards away. "Are we getting ready to start filming, Superman? Things got so slow."

"We're heading somewhere else," I replied. "To another movie about an hour from here."

"What are you talking about?" she asked.

This caught Chaim's attention.

"Another movie?" he asked. "We don't have time for two movies."

"No, the other movie starts just about when this movie finishes," I explained. "That Greek assistant director brought it to my attention and asked if I wanted to check it out with him. He's going now and has a car. You two are invited if you want to come along with me and Sandra. An hour's ride from here. The director of that movie is there doing whatever. Prelim stuff, I suppose. We're going to see if he has room for us in the movie."

"I came to Korea to see another culture," Chaim said with a grin. "Turns out I'm seeing more of the Hollywood culture than the Far East."

"Exactly," I concurred. "Are you game?"

"Sure," Chaim and Sunshine said in unison.

"Thanks for thinking of us," Chaim said.

"You got it all started, Chaim. So there. Karma can be good too, you know, not just payback. Or it can be good payback too, not just bad karma."

Freddy was very knowledgeable concerning the insides of the movie industry and talked about it the entire drive. His entire being seemed wrapped around the mystique and mechanics of Hollywood.

"Do you aspire to be an actor, Wilson?" he asked me during the conversation.

"Not really," I answered. "Sometimes, growing up, it had an appeal, but I mostly wanted academics. I love history, in particular. I want to learn and teach."

"You could do research for motion pictures, you know. They always need accuracy. Movies sensationalize a great deal, but there still needs to be factual basis in a story. The movie public can be unforgiving if you get your facts wrong."

"It's a nice medium to educate the masses," I said. "But yes, there is too much fudging of the data, of truth itself, in a story. Novels too. Sometimes even history books fudge the truth. I guess 'slant the truth' is a better term. I'd rather work with the real meat of history. The data, the facts. If a storyteller wants to alter history to entertain or to brainwash, that's their business. But I want to be the one they reference for the truth."

"So movies are out for you," he surmised. "I hope you change your mind. You've got potential. I'd like to see you give it a shot. I can pretend I had something to do with making you into something."

The area of our destination was desolate. We detoured onto small highways, then onto a narrow dirt road. There was only a van and a car parked by a wooden cottage when we arrived.

"Good afternoon," a middle-aged man greeted us as we entered his quarters.

"Good afternoon," Freddy returned. "I'm glad you are here, after all it took to find this location. I told you about Wilson. I told him I would let him meet the director of a new movie to be made. We brought some of his ambitious friends. We're hoping you have something."

"Well, you may be in luck. The funding for the picture is adequate. The script is finished. An American GI falls in love with a local, but culture and politics hamper their attempts to get married. Same thing happened in Japan after World War II. We are already casting for some of the parts. We will need some Americans."

"Chaim here is Israeli," Freddy informed him.

"You mean he has an accent."

"Yes, sir, I do," Chaim acknowledged.

"And we have a Swede," Freddy acknowledged further.

"But she doesn't have an accent," I said. "She sounds more American than we do."

"She looks like an actress," the director of interest said approvingly.

"Yes, indeed she does," Freddy agreed, grinning broadly.

"Listen," the director said. "Give me your business

cards. We'll have a place for you. I'm sure of it. Small parts. But we'll see how you turn out. Who knows."

"We're all stragglers and extras," I intervened. "Just passing through. We don't have any business cards."

The director tore off a piece of notebook paper from a pad he had in his shirt pocket. He then pulled out a ballpoint pen.

"Just write your names on this piece of paper," he instructed. "I already have Freddy's vitals from his friend working with us. I'll keep all of yours together in my wallet until I get to my hotel room. I'll enter them in my logbook. I'll know how to reach you through the movie you're doing. It may be a couple of weeks, however."

"Fine," Freddy replied as he passed the piece of paper to me. "The movie we work with now should be finished by then."

The director inspected our names, then folded the piece of paper before stuffing it into his wallet. He then looked at us.

"I know how to reach Freddy here, as I said. I'll let him know shortly if things are a go. He can inform the rest of you. Thank you for offering your time. Have a good return trip."

"To the point," Freddy said with a chuckle as he held out his hand to the director.

None of us spoke as we walked back to the car. Soon, subtle grins appeared on our faces as the impact of our meeting brought out a celebratory feeling.

"This can be fun," Freddy said as we drove back to Pusan. "For all the frustrations and rejections involved in the movie world, even a crumb like this makes our efforts seem rewarding."

He looked over at me and nodded his head approvingly.

"It's the challenge," he explained. "As much as the job itself, it's the challenge that keeps me going."

He nodded again for emphasis.

Chapter 20

"Do you know who sang that?" inquired our British friend as he looked up from his guitar. He scoped us out one at a time as a challenge.

"Who?" the Frenchman finally asked. "I have heard the song somewhere. Thousands of years ago, perhaps."

"Elvis Presley," the Brit answered with a grin.

"No," the Dutch girl blurted out. "That was so good. I forgot he sang such good songs."

"Back in his early days," the Brit explained. "He really was that good."

"Okay, move on," the Frenchman suggested. "New blood. Our new Aussie friend now. Initiation rites are in order. Sing us a song from Down Under."

"Tie Me Kangaroo Down," the Dutch girl said with a laugh.

"Too corny," the guy from Nepal broke in. "Even for me."

"I know an Australian song," I said.

"Give Superman here the guitar, then," the Brit said as he handed it to me.

I loved this song and was glad for the excuse to sing it. But as I sang, solemn looks took hold of everyone. Was I that bad, or did the song bore them?

"Blimey, mate," the Aussie groaned after I finished singing. "Only our corny songs seem to make it to the front. That's a kid's song, down in Oz."

"The Seekers sang it," I came back.

"Even worse," the Aussie complained further. "That's what they do. Kid songs. Folk songs. Corny, corny, corny. What the world settles for. Forget the Seekers. Let's hear some Sex Pistols, Brits that they are."

"Sing what you want," I said with a bite. "I don't care. We have folk songs too. Everyone does. I like this song."

"I suppose you like 'Home On The Range' then," the Aussie said pointedly.

"I love 'Home On The Range,' " I returned.

Everyone stared at me in disbelief, including Sandra.

"There it is, mate," the Brit said with a snicker. "That is a bleeding kid's song. I'll stay out of Aussie domain. I don't know this song just sung, but 'Home On The Range,' even though it's Texan, or whatever it is, is universal for a kid's song. Even *the* kid's song. He's got you, mate."

I grimaced. I hated these arguments. But I also cherished them.

"So that settles that," I sneered. "They teach it in grade school or on Captain Kangaroo or wherever, and that's the end of it for you. It became so commonplace through the years because it is so beautiful. Simple but beautiful. So, all these years later, it's for kids. Not to be taken seriously as a song or for culture."

"Culture, you say?" the Aussie groaned. "And what the bleedin' hell is beautiful about it? Because it talks about buffalo and antelope? Back to nature stuff? We can meditate under a tree, if you like."

"And we grow up and move on to drugs, sex, and rock and roll," I countered. "Yes, let's get back to nature as some counterculture visual, but the real deal bores you. I love the wide-open spaces back home where the buffalo *do* still run free. I don't know what you do with your deserts and wilderness back in Oz, but I love our open prairies and how they inspire songs like this. I don't mind kids being taught them—it's great to learn as a kid. But we still have a lot of forests and deserts and coastline environments, and these songs still fit. You don't have to smoke dope to like them or to get back to nature as some drug high. And the second verse to 'Home On The Range' goes even further than the first for tranquil beauty."

"I didn't know it had a second verse," the Frenchman broke in.

"It does," I replied. "I don't know how it got lost."

"So give it to us, then," the Brit challenged. "God forgive me for dragging this out."

I found my key for it and began. I chose to focus on the guitar as I sang, not wanting to see their reactions to the song.

The Frenchman nodded his head in satisfaction after I finished singing.

"That is beautiful," he commented. "It truly is. Our Texan is right."

"It is, mate," the Brit seconded.

"I never heard that verse before," Sandra said. "The second verse. I didn't know there was a second verse either. It makes sense there is, but all these years later, I never even thought about it. Yes, we're taught all this as a child and then move on. That was beautiful, though."

"Good visual, Superman," the Aussie said with an approving smile. "From the heart. I'm sure the first verse also was touching originally, but it is so stuffy now. You made your point."

"Superman," one of the Korean girls said with a smile, "I know this song, but not so well as to know if it is for children. It has good feelings and words. I like more such songs, please."

The Aussie looked around the group of us as if inspired.

"This was refreshing," he swooned. "The words were as if to God. Yes, the words have you visualize as you look to the heavens like in the song, not just seeing the stars but in touch with them. And with appreciation to the creator. I'm glad we never heard the second verse before. Somehow it too may have gotten stale with redundancy."

"These nights here at the hostel are perfect," Sunshine said with a sigh. "Mates, that's what the world is missing. Mates. We're all mates here. Each of us with a perspective to share."

"To be shared as we do each night here," the Brit concurred. "Wonderful to be here. It really is. It's so wonderful to be here in Korea like this with each of you."

Chapter 21

"We have been here just over a month," Sandra said to me at our lunch break on the set, "and we have not done any research for our thesis, yours or mine, the whole time. Unless you count the movie and what we think we've learned from the plot in it. None of which will classify as primary data, you know."

"I'm aware of it," I responded. "I haven't forgotten. We're here, and the movie is giving us a background. But we can't even access the profs Maria was to introduce to us. I never saw her again. So what we need to do is drive around and visit sites and universities when the movie is over. The movie is wrapping up now. We'll get it done."

"We're not waiting for the movie to end," she returned sharply. "We've dragged our feet enough already. It turns out we need our one day off from the movie just to rest. But no more. Tomorrow's Sunday, and I want to go somewhere now, Wilson. As in tonight. We'll have to rent a car. I can borrow my mother's car, but we'd waste time retrieving it. Cars are cheap here. We're on the southern tip of the South Korean coast. It's a small country. We'll drive to Janggok tonight. That's near the North Korean border. There's an Army base nearby there. Tourist agencies arrange guided tours. I want to see more of this country. We've only been in the southern part."

"How much are we going to cover of the war, then, in our one day out?" I asked her. "We need to write about Pusan and what happened here. Our research is here."

"But we have to mention the rest of the war at least some. As a reference."

"A guided tour isn't primary data," I reminded her.

"But it will highlight what we want to note about the rest of the war. I want to see some of this country, and the tour will help us choose what we research later on. So let's do this."

"I feel like I owe my committee chairman an apology," I said as an afterthought.

"Why?" Sandra asked. She then withdrew in thought. "Yeah," she said with a sigh. "Yeah. Right on. We've been slackers. And here we go on a tour. A damn tour. Ha. That'll be the most research we've done privately while we're here. The rest as extras in a damn Hollywood movie. We're pathetic."

"It's your fault, Sandra."

She let out a laugh.

"How's that, kiddo? Explain how this is my fault. You're the one who entered my life and dragged me into this movie."

"Dragged you? Dragged you, you say? If you hadn't pestered me about being in this movie when I first met you, I would have gotten something done. Instead, I've been shacking up with you and having a sex holiday. I'll never get my Master's now. I can't keep my mind off of you. Between Hollywood and hot romance, I've barely even thought about my thesis."

She let out a chuckle, turned directly toward me, and wrapped her arms around my neck.

"Well, you have a point there, Mr. Superman, you. I have the hots for you, and it's made a disastrous detour in my future, as well."

"What future is that?" I asked her. "Are you asking me to marry you? Then I'd have to transfer to West Texas State."

"No, I didn't bring up marriage. And if that happened, I'd just transfer to A&M."

Suddenly we grew quiet.

"How did we get on this conversation, Sandra? Is this Freudian, or why are we talking so seriously all of a sudden? We've only known each other a month."

"Two months," she came back.

"A month and a half is closer."

We stared at each other for a moment, unable to find any more words.

"Were we joking just now?" she asked me straightforwardly.

"I don't know. How did we get onto marriage? It hasn't even crossed my mind."

"Then how did it come up?"

"I guess it's been on my mind after all."

"We can't get married, Wilson. Seriously. We're both in the middle of our education. Two different schools, too. And we've only known each other a couple of months."

I nodded my head and chewed nervously on my lower lip.

"We were having fun," I said as an explanation attempt. "It was fun. But kind of scary."

"Why scary?"

"Because I enjoy the thought of marrying you."

She pulled down on me to kiss me.

"Me too. But listen, my dear. We know we have to go slow. But going slow let us live in denial about our relationship, it seems. Remember our talks before? About going slow, you know? We just now made our relationship more serious than it was meant to be. So I'm not putting any genie back in the bottle, but let's just ride the waves a bit longer, now that we've acknowledged how serious each of us feels. We'll know more about us when the movie ends in a couple of weeks. And then we'll see what our studies present to us—regrets or longing, you know. Probably we're going to move into second gear now, since the idea is appealing. A post-Korea us to think about and how we cope with that. I won't bring this up to my parents when we get to Seoul after the movie. We'll want to do some research in libraries while we're there, since that's why we came to Korea in the first place. If we're still serious, or more serious, we can talk it over with my parents before we go back to Texas."

"Sounds like a plan," I chided.

"Best one for now," she replied.

We stared at one another a bit longer.

"So let's go on that tour at the Demilitarized Zone," she beckoned. "The DMZ. We do need the distraction."

"Yeah," I said. "Yeah."

Sandra's gaze my way turned starry-eyed.

"Wilson, I'm happy. This Freudian slip of ours has made me very happy." She rubbed my cheek, then kissed me yet again. "Hey, let's go get that car before we get distracted yet again,"

We found a cheap rental on base, then began our quest for the DMZ. Just for the doing. Research only made it official as an excuse to get out. South Korea was small, but still somewhat underdeveloped. We had to fight traffic much of the way.

"Here is a hostel," Sandra said as she pointed to a small building.

"It's a bed-and-breakfast," I corrected.

"Good enough. Let's pack it in. Get some supper and some sleep. We'll catch the DMZ tomorrow."

It was a small village just outside of Janggok where we stayed. I wanted small. I was in no mood for hassles.

"This is a nice restaurant," Sandra commented from our small wooden table.

"It's small," I said. "I'm glad we chose it. They need the business. Family owned. They make home cooked. Like mama."

"If you like squid and fried rice," she teased. "Our mamas didn't make much of that."

"It feels so good to get out," I commented. "I can't believe we didn't do this before."

"We were caught up in our life. Especially with all the new characters from around the world at the hostel. Always somebody new coming and going. And the Korean college girls looking for a quick pick-up, too. Entertaining to watch the hormones in all this."

"Yeah," I replied. "Yeah, that's what kept us from going out. We lived in a microcosm of our own right there at the hostel."

"But finally, we got out. And were ready for it. The timing was right."

"Except we're out of time now for our research."

"We abused Korea," she said, looking guilty. "I was sure I would see more places. We're not going to have time to see much of Korea now. We can from where my parents live, but still, we blew it."

"I have no regrets, though, Sandra. We'll have to put the study into high gear, for sure. Like cramming for a final. But between the movie, the Hollywood crowd, and our friends at the hostel, I can't regret anything."

"From here on out, though, Wilson, we're researching. For my conscience."

I nodded.

"The research starts tomorrow," she continued. "From here on out. We have to find a place to hole up for our Sundays more often. To study something about a place. Or at least a library around. We've got our bearings now. We'll get our research done. Even back in Seoul."

With these assurances, we slept at our coziest. Right in the small lodge the restaurant family owned. Tomorrow was another day for us.

"Welcome, everyone," a husky American tour guide greeted us as we boarded a bus in Janggok the next morning. "We will include some history of Korea as we show you around today, most particularly relating to the divide of the country, both geographically as well as culturally of late. We will also take you to the border with North Korea at the Demilitarized Zone. We will even include a brief visit inside North Korea itself."

He let that shocking statement sink in for a moment before smiling.

"We have an agreement with the government of North Korea where a room we will visit juts out into North Korean territory ever so slightly. You will be allowed to set foot there and be able to brag about it to your friends back home."

Sandra and I turned to one another to celebrate this joyful news.

"The Kingdom of Korea," our guide explained further, "was begun as early as the seventh century BC, according to Chinese records. The name Korea itself is derived from the word Goguryeo. At times, it was considered one of the great powers of East Asia, not just ruling most of what is today the Korean peninsula, but also parts of Manchuria, and parts of what is now the Russian Far East, as well as inner Mongolia."

With this background, suddenly Korea held character and prominence for me. There was so much more to Korea than I'd heard or imagined. This tour reminded me why I loved history.

The guide kept the lecture brief, barely twenty minutes, knowing the limited attention spans of most tourists. I was aware from my Asian history classes in college how it was conquered by the expanding Japanese empire in 1910. I wondered why he didn't bring that up. He talked mostly of the one thing that seemingly everyone knew about Korea, the war in 1950 that began when the Communists invaded the southern half of the Korean peninsula. This schism left the country as Communist in the North, aligned with the Soviet Union and China, while the southern half of the peninsula was aligned with the United States, as Sandra and I had experienced first-hand.

As much as history intrigued me, however, the exciting part of the tour was when we were allowed to set foot in the small portion of North Korea that was included in the building we visited.

"So you see the soldier," our guide explained as he

pointed. "That is a North Korean Communist on the other side of this glass enclosure. He is not there to keep you out. This bulletproof glass wall we are confronting does that. He is there to demonstrate how this indeed is North Korea where we are staring. With his menacing look he is a symbol of North Korean strength and temperament. They don't like us. We are the enemy. We are not welcomed. We would be welcomed only as enlightened subjects of the center of virtue known as the Democratic People's Republic of Korea."

"Democratic," one of the tourists in our group said with a laugh. "All these Commie countries are quote unquote democratic republics. They willingly choose to be slaves of tyranny."

"The South had its own problems with democracy," the guide replied. "Democracy, in general, is a new concept to most of the world. It did get an early start in places like ancient Greece, but letting the masses choose their own form of government is a tricky business that our own forefathers in America had suspicions about. They weren't sure our republic would survive, only that it was an idea whose time had come, and they were going to set up the structures and guidelines for it. So here in South Korea they also have problems with setting up a republic. It is basically a republic in name only, in the South, just like with the North Koreans. I don't really mean just like the North. I much prefer living here rather than in the harshness and brutality of North Korea, but the South doesn't live up to being a republic either."

"They have a dictatorship," I said out loud.

The guide nodded his head in agreement.

"It comes close to dictatorship at times," he said. "Until recently, Korea was a kingdom or was ruled by foreign powers. And I mentioned already about the Korean War and events leading up to it, with Cold War tensions between the Soviet Union and the United States as a result. With Communism bearing down on their part of the world from Russia, then China, political and ideological tensions formed, as a result, all over the peninsula known as Korea, as you know. When the breakup of what had been a unified country occurred, the South was not an eager conduit for democracy, in spite of its relationship with America. The reason we backed the South's dictator, to be blunt about Syngman Rhee, is because Rhee hated Communists and Communism. He was our pick of a dictator. We literally picked him to head a provisional government, in fact, until elections could take place. We would have loved for there to be truth, democracy, and the American way here, but you don't force democracy on anyone even if you arrange elections for the possibility. They had not yet evolved into a democratic mindset, even with the election of Syngman Rhee to head a provisional government. The Soviets got involved and declared their guy in the North, Kim Il-Sung, as grand and glorious leader of all Korea. That created problems, as we well know with the resulting Korean War."

"The war is technically still on, isn't it?" I asked the guide.

"That is correct," he answered. "There is no physical military confrontation anymore, overall anyway, but the previous state of war is still in existence. There is an armistice, but South Korea never signed it. So."

"A split in the peninsula along the Demilitarized Zone, the DMZ," another tourist added, "that's as close as we got to working things out. A DMZ created and physical war put on hold."

"That's correct," the guide acknowledged. "The gist of it, anyway."

"So finish about Syngman Rhee," another tourist came in.

"Yes," the guide stated. "That affects things today. South Korea needs strength, and they came up with a strongman for that, instead of true democracy, which they weren't fully in tune with anyway, due to their past. More Korean civilians died in the Korean War in the early 1950s, proportionally, than there were civilian deaths in World War II or in the later Vietnam conflict. All the major cities in Korea were destroyed. So they needed strength. Despots don't often work out well, but there was a need for strength, and they got Syngman Rhee as a result. He was deposed in a student uprising in 1960. Our backing a strongman also created animosity toward us with many South Koreans, especially students. They expected more from us than to back a despot. The best-laid plans, as they say. That's world politics, and you play the hand dealt you."

Sandra and I looked at one another with our eyes dancing. This was not the research vehicle we came to Korea to attain, but it got our focus placed on our mission once again.

"I can hardly wait for the movie to end now," I told Sandra on our drive back to Pusan.

"And seeing North Korea physically at the DMZ," she said with a fake shiver. "That highlights my whole time here somehow."

"And that North Korean guard staring hate at us from the glass wall? That was real."

"He was expressionless," she corrected. "He didn't stare hate at us."

"It was more than a neutral soldier's monotone stare," I said. "He was grim. He hated us."

"Let's do our research together," she said excitedly. "It won't feel like a thesis."

"We're waiting for the movie to be finished so we can go back to the entertainment of formal education. We're pathetic, you know."

"That we are," she answered with a wink.

"Watch the road," I instructed, "or you'll get us killed."

"So we're not going to make that other movie then?" she asked. "We're not going to be Hollywood stars after all. Just dull, boring academics for the rest of our pathetic lives?"

"That's the easy part to decide. The hard part is finding out how we're going to spend that life together."

Chapter 22

"This movie is so much fun," Sandra said to me our first day back on the set. "I know we get bored a lot too, but I don't mind making it at all. Even though it distracted us from our research. We were only gone Sunday, our one day off, but it was a different world while we did that. Going to the DMZ and our first bit of research, if that's what you call it, put me back in my place. Our place, I'm assuming. Meaning our thesis, which we are shamelessly ignoring. But what a blast while we're ignoring it. So I guess I'm more focused now. Enjoying everyone while making the movie, and now reorienting to research too."

"I know what you mean," I said with a nod. "Yeah. The movie's been fun, but a distraction, even though it is about the subject matter we came here for. But I don't regret any of this about making the movie with our friends. It's energized me. And I got intimate with you. Fate, you know."

"Fate," she said with a chuckle. "I'll go with that. I didn't think I believed in that, but here we are. So I'll go along with fate."

Our conversation was interrupted by a commotion headed our way. Five young helmeted Marines barged into our movie set environment most brashly. They were loud, obnoxious, and wearing arrogant smiles. We, along with the soldiers on the set, turned our focus on them.

"This must be where we belong, Gunny," one of the men said to a tall, muscular, black Marine with two rockers under his sergeant stripes.

"We'll wait to see what they want with us," the gunnery sergeant said. He exuded self-confidence.

"We're the only Marines here," another of the men in the group said. "If all they need is numbers for some extravaganza we're to be part of, I guess they got them. If they need to kick some Commie ass, though, they don't need these wimps. The Marines have landed. Realism has arrived. But I guess Hollywood doesn't care."

The Marines in the group looked around. Contempt showed on their faces as they scoped out the soldiers and airmen in their midst.

"Who are these guys?" Sandra said in amazement. "They're geared to take over, I think."

"Boy, they idolize their gunnery sergeant," I commented. "He's cool, calm, and collected. He'll control them."

A smile eased on Sandra's face.

"You hear about racism," she mused. "Not here. They idolize their sergeant."

"Yeah, they do," I replied. "He's like some Greek god to them. He's in charge, for sure. I guess it's fun for them to be here, and a few extra bucks too."

"I don't know if fun is the word. They seem like it's beneath them to be here."

"Wilson," one of the assistant directors called out as he walked up to me. I looked his direction. "You need to work with the stuntmen just now. They're in another area. I'll take you."

"What about Sandra?" I asked him.

He thought for a moment, then nodded.

"Yes. Yes. There will be a need for some women. We may have enough already, but bring her along, and some of the other girls, too."

"Sunshine," Sandra called out to our friend a few yards away. "Come with us. We're needed on another set."

"We're needed?" Sunshine asked curiously. "Who is we?"

"You and any of the girls in our group that you see. But come now, or we'll get left behind."

"What exactly are we going to do?" I asked the assistant director as he waited on the girls.

"You and the other stuntmen are going to rescue a mission school in the middle of a village. You're part of a special squad. Thus, we don't need the larger Army groups here. Only a special forces type of squad. It's an action scene."

"Eight of us are going to take a village?" I asked him.

"We'll need a few more," the assistant director answered. "But not too many. Like I said, it's an action scene. Drama and heroics. Not a full battle."

"I got some guys for you," I said.

"What are you talking about?" the assistant asked.

"There's five combat-ready Marines just over there," I said, pointing. "They'll fit in an action scene and look authentic too."

The assistant director scoped them out and nodded his head.

"Yes, they look good," he praised. "Authentic. Believable, I mean. You know, over what we've been dealing with so far. Bring them with you," he instructed. "Meet me over at that truck by the coffee stand. Where we got off this morning when we arrived. We'll be leaving in fifteen minutes. We won't be coming back here. We'll go back to town on our own later this afternoon."

"Sure," I replied. "Let me get them."

I walked over to the Marines of interest that we'd just admired.

"Y'all here for a purpose?" I asked the gunny.

"We got the day off to be extras for this movie," he answered. "We took leave to get it. We heard about it and wanted to get involved. A good memory, you know."

"It's as close to combat as we're going to get these days," one of the Marines in the group complained. "Kick some ass Hollywood-style, maybe."

"I got a place for you," I told them. "We're going to be a special squad to rescue a school. Y'all look more combat ready than these other guys around. I'm one of the stuntmen. There's eight of us, and we need a few more."

"Special forces," one of the Marines howled. "Get some. Kick some ass."

"A mission to save a school," another Marine celebrated. "That's what we came here for. We're going to be in a movie, you damn grunts. Not as good as live combat, but saved on the silver screen. That'll do for now."

"Follow me," I instructed. "There's a truck waiting on us."

"Bust some heavies," one of the Marines cheered. "Whooh doggies. I'll get an Oscar."

"Come." I beckoned.

They followed while still celebrating along the way.

"Here they are," I told the assistant director when we arrived.

"All right. Get on the truck there. We'll be leaving soon. The girls are already on the truck."

"Girls?" One of the Marines swooned with sparkling eyes.

"Yeah, Godzilla," another teased him. "Be on your best manners."

"Manners?" the first Marine came back.

It made me long to be in the service as we rode the truck. These Marines made a good time out of everything. And the way they couldn't help themselves from stealing glances at our female companions added to the good time. The testosterone was abundant.

"So, Wilson," the assistant director who was with us instructed me, "this scene will be short but to the point. Take our special forces team here to the abandoned Army tank in front of us. Hide behind it until I give you the cue. All I'll do is shout out, 'Go now, Wilson.' Motion for the team to run out screaming into the road here. Have your rifles ready to fire. But by your side. You're running. You won't fire unless fired upon, which won't happen in this scene. We just need the dramatics. That's all. A fire team charging is all you do. We'll fill in the rest of the scene later and rescue the girls being held in the school also. Uneventful, but it often is."

I nodded my head in agreement. Hollywood was often more boring than dramatic, for sure.

Waiting for our cue to charge from behind the tank

took an hour. It seemed like all day. When given the go ahead, we charged and screamed until our faces turned red. The entire segment lasted not even a minute long.

"That's it?" one of the Marines in our group asked me in disbelief after our endeavor was complete. "We drive all the way out here, all geared up, all ready to save the world, and all we do is run out in the road screaming. An instant of fame and that's it? Finito? I'll never bother watching another movie. Who cares about all this?"

"It's like painting a Rembrandt," I analyzed aloud. "A coat of base on an empty canvas, then a smudge of paint here and there, a touch of color or shade to fill in, and next thing you know you have glorious art in a museum that everyone admires."

The Marine shook his head in disgust. He wasn't buying it. Hollywood and movies sucked.

Chapter 23

"Wasn't that another of your cowboy folk songs?" the Brit asked me at our evening social interchange.

"Yes," I replied.

"You seem to like them," the Frenchman commented. "Somewhere in your singing to us you always throw in another one. 'Ghost Riders In The Sky,' isn't it? I hate to call it a kid's song after you redirected our attitudes about those with 'Home On The Range' before."

"I love these songs," I replied, "these old folk songs and cowboy songs. And yes, they were taught to us as kids, which got them trite to us early on in our childhood. Enjoyable and worth singing, but trite. The words here in this one really stir me, though. They are anything but trite. Not just a fairy tale. Moving."

"Steers snorting fire and all that nonsense," the Aussie interjected. "Kid's stuff. Fun, but kid's stuff. Go ahead, Texas man, straighten me out. Convince me I should take this song seriously. It is fun, but for kids."

"That's how these songs made it into our lives," I explained. "As folk songs or not. They had value in their day and could again. They should. That's why they're still here. But we use them as singalongs or to teach our kids for amusement."

"I like them, Superman," one of the Korean girls in our midst praised.

"You are a funny one, Wilson," the Dutch girl said. "Enjoyable, but you take things so seriously."

"He's working on his Master's degree in history," Sandra answered in my defense. "These songs focus you on the details of the times. Not just some date to memorize, like Columbus discovered the New World in 1492. Wilson has an intuition about such things. That's why he's into history and cultures. They are more than ornaments to the likes of him and to myself."

"Did you ever listen to the words?" I asked to back her up. "Just like I brought up with 'Home On The Range.' To have to memorize 1492 as an important date is necessary but boring. A chore. Unless you capture what it all means. Then you don't have to memorize. You gladly remember because it matters to you. 1492 was the year Ferdinand and Isabella of Spain kicked out all the Jews. The Muslim Moors were freshly conquered, and all foreign influence was reduced or turned away. Jews were subjected to the Inquisition and forced to convert to Christianity, to Catholicism in particular, or they were exiled or killed. Some say Columbus himself may have been Jewish and was desperate to find a new world for Jews to flee to. I have no idea if that's true. But it all sends chills up my spine to picture it. I love this stuff. I don't memorize. It becomes part of me. It doesn't take memorization to remember what entices you. It's pure joy. Like a great novel, except it's real."

Everyone stared at Sandra as if to see her take on what I said.

"Yes," Sandra reinforced. "I love history for that. The perspective of life. Of cultures. Art, politics, science. It gives the present meaning. Like our own past, our growing up, does for our life now. Or knowing about our parents being in the Depression, or immigrating from Europe, or Asia, or wherever. It adds to life more than just waking up in the morning and trying to get by for another day. So I like the way Wilson listens to songs the way he does, and for the meaning behind them if it's there in a song."

"I'm from Texas," I came in. "Rural Texas, even. So I identify with some cowpoke on his horse riding along on the prairie. Nice start to the song. But then across the sky comes a lost herd of cattle. Fairytale for kids, I know, but it isn't. It's his psyche. His soul. Or from God directly. But something is getting his attention. His spiritual attention. Something to expand his life, his search, or to start a search."

"You are a strange one, Superman," the Dutch girl insisted. "I never cared. I still don't, but keep going. All this from a kid's song."

"There's vast open spaces in Texas," I continued.

"Like in Australia," the Aussie broke in.

"Yes, comparable," I said. "I grew up in the southern tip of Texas. By Mexico. But my parents came from the West Texas plains. We'd have family reunions and travel five hundred miles to get to West Texas. We'd travel at night some, too. Less traffic and not as hot. So miles and miles sometimes of nothing but miles. We called it 'the great alone.' I loved it. You can hear God. So here's this cowpoke in this song, and it's nothing but him and God. Either you literally believe there was a ghost herd he encountered, or it was God speaking to him, a troubled soul. There's still this imagery. It's more than a story. There's something to identify with in our own way."

"I can't identify with a cowpoke confronting a herd of ghost cattle," the Frenchman said with a laugh.

"Then don't. But something in you can in other ways, or you'll get nothing out of this song. Let it be just a kid's song to you then, if you prefer. But the lonely part of any of us can identify in some way with this song. Where our conscience demands from us more than we've been."

"Ou-la-la," the Frenchman scoffed. "You should have been a priest."

"I'd rather be a cowboy," I came back.

"Let him finish," the Brit said. "I want to hear."

"There was a herd of cattle, as if trapped spirits from Hell. You know, the psyche. This is what dreams do. Dreams are often not literal but poetic. This ghost herd is chased by cowboys who were doomed to eternity to do this. But not just chase. The cattle were from Hell, the horses the cowboys rode snorted fire. And the cowboys were doomed for eternity to chase this ghost herd. Hell in the cowboy culture, you might say."

"A cowboy take on the biblical Hell," the Frenchman commented in agreement.

"But not a fairy tale," I reiterated. "A spiritual truth. It's so beautiful. Piercing. God talks to us through our own medium. So, even the biblical imagery can be customized for people like me. Whether there is a biblical Hell or not in a literal way, the spirit of the message is real. One of the cowboys chasing the ghost herd stops to look at the cowboy on the prairie looking at all of this. Something is eating at this cowboy beholding the ghost riders. And his soul demands he listen. And the cowboy from the group of those chasing the cattle looks directly at him. The cowboy who is doomed to this cowboy version of Hell looks at our hero cowboy down on the prairie and tells him, 'If you want to save yourself, then hear.' I love it. God speaks to us in ways we have to listen to. In our own language."

"Yes, yes," our Nepalese friend interrupted. "For sure, this is the purpose of art. To entertain or to speak to us. Like literature, but the melody of this song is very eery. As are the words. This is art at its best. To cheer us up, to make us happy, or sad. Or to speak to our conscience like some Bob Dylan song. It uses our own culture to speak. Your Bible brought to terms with your own culture and conscience. I am Buddhist. We do the same thing. It is nice to hear this from a kid's song. So I see how Superman is thinking. Why he is upset that a song with so much meaning became like a fixture to pass down in your culture but then gets so trivialized by that culture. Yes, that is wonderful to hear him explain it like he does. I so love our time together and all that we share."

"Yes, me too," the Dutch girl said with a sigh. "I will never forget our group."

Things became silent as we reflected together.

"So are you two going to get married here?" our Aussie friend asked as he focused on Sandra and myself. "In Korea, in particular Pusan, so we can all go to it?"

The question caught me by surprise. To stall in answering the question, I looked at Sandra for help.

"We don't take such thoughts seriously," she replied. "Getting married, I mean. We do get caught up at times, fantasizing. I hate to say even that. Afraid to egg you on with this suggestion. Our relationship up to now is just day to day. Falling in love. Having fun. Experiencing. Not just our romance, but experiencing everyone here, as well. All part of Korea itself to us. Like the movie. But suddenly, we're getting married, you're asking? Ha. That's too easy. I don't know what all we will do about our lives or how we'll do it."

I looked at our friend to see if that answered things.

"So, then," he returned, "if you haven't really thought about it, but sense you might want to do this, get married, then do it here. It will highlight our time together here. A cherished remembrance to go along with all the other cherished memories we have. I only just got here a month ago, but I already feel so attached to everyone. Between our great communal outings here at the hostel, and then, of course, making a movie together. What an experience! Just a thought there, mate. Don't do it for us. Unless you really are going to get married, then do it here for us."

"That's right," the Frenchman seconded.

"Yes, yes," the Nepalese concurred. "That would be magnificent. What a treat for us all!"

"Right on," the Brit added.

"Oh, yes," the Korean girls swooned.

Sandra and I studied each other with the thought.

"It is a nice idea," I commented. "We haven't adjusted to the idea. Like Sandra said, we've only flirted with it."

"Aha," the Aussie bellowed. "So there. You have thought about it."

"Not sure of yourself, then," the Dutch girl teased.

Sandra took a deep breath.

"One has to be sure," she said. "We have feelings,

154

for sure."

"Don't push them so hard," Sunshine said sympathetically. "Enough marriages fail. Let them go their own pace about this. To really see."

"I suppose," the Brit said. "But we get to be disappointed. The movie soon ends. This would be a great topping off of events."

"See," Sunshine admonished. "It's exciting for us. But we don't have to make such a decision. To want to get married, to plan to marry, it needs more than an exciting time."

"You're right," the Dutch girl said. "One needs to be sure of something like this."

"Getting married sounds swell," I broke in. "That's part of the problem. And we're both from Texas. Just a little too easy to feel snug about all of this."

"Marry her, Superman," a Korean girl said with a sigh.

"What's so big about this?" the Frenchman scoffed. "There are military bases right here, as we all know since we enter the compounds of one every day. They have chaplains. They can advise. Let's do this. What a party for us!"

"Ou-la-la!" The Aussie laughed out. "A party is it, now?"

"Sounds nice," I said, dreamy-eyed. "Makes me want to look into it. If we're going to do this, we better get cracking, though. There are always complications and holdups."

"Wilson," Sandra gasped. "We've talked about this, and you know we're not ready."

"What's not ready, Sandra?" I countered. "I'm ready."

"You weren't, just last night," she answered with a bite.

"I needed to adjust to the idea," I replied.

"Did you make amour beyond all ecstasy?" the Frenchman said with a laugh. "Superman woke up a new man, it seems, and now wants to make the plunge into wedding bliss. Such a night!"

Sandra looked down at the ground, then back at me. A smile spread on her face, and she nodded yes to my suggestion.

"That's the spirit, blokes," the Aussie celebrated.

"Is that okay with you, then?" I asked her.

Her smile broadened.

"It sounds exciting," she said. "I love the thought. Yes, let's do this. Get married right here and share it with all our friends. To be honest, I've wanted to marry Wilson since our first week of living together. It felt so domestically wonderful. I kept talking myself out of it, though. Yes, so many marriages fail. And here we are half way around the world. All the more reason to not fully trust these feelings. Like holiday spirit feelings, too much, I fear. But what a wonderful send-off for us to be with you if we get married. Somehow we're— poof!—betrothed and no one asked anyone to get married. Wilson didn't ask me, anyway."

"Do it, man," the Brit coaxed. "Get on your bleedin' knee and propose to the lass."

"Beg her hand," a Korean girl beckoned.

"Yes," the Dutch girl seconded. "Do it. Right here. Get on your knee, Superman."

I loved the thought of getting married to Sandra. I took to one knee.

"He's doing it," Sunshine yelped. "He's getting on

his knee. Right here."

"Would you give me the honor," I asked Sandra, "of being my wife?"

Sandra reached for one of my hands.

"Wait," she replied. There was silence for several seconds. "Sorry," she said in a quivering voice. "I'm getting emotional now."

"God love you, *ma chère*," the Frenchman said.

"I would be honored to be your wife, Wilson," she answered as she looked me in the eyes.

"That's the spirit," the Brit said as he walked over to hug us. "Then we'll decide where to go for our honeymoon. I say Hawaii."

"Aahgh," Sunshine groaned. "You are pathetic. But yeah, let's go on the honeymoon too. All of us together."

Sandra and I broke out in laughter. The owner of the hostel perked up as he listened.

"You marry here?" he asked. "In Korea? Then you marry here in my hostel. Yes, we marry you here. We make happy wedding here. That good idea. I make very wonderful food for you. For all. We have great wedding. Right here. When marry, then?"

"My God," I let out in an exaggerated sigh. "Whew, what's happened all of a sudden?"

"Let them breathe," Sunshine sympathized.

"No, no," the Brit said. "We want a bleedin' marriage. Right here, right now."

"I make you good wedding," the hostel owner promised. "You have wonderful memory for all your life. Marry right here Korea. You find love here and you marry here. Right here."

"Yeah, the bloke's right," the Aussie said. "We'll

find the fastest legal way to get married, and we'll all be a part of it. You'll remember this the rest of your lives, and so will we."

"My parents are here," Sandra mused. "In Seoul, anyway. It's easy to get them here."

I looked at her incredulously.

"Are we really going to get married here now?" I asked her as the full force of the moment hit. "I mean as soon as we get it all formalized?"

"Yes, Wilson," she said seductively just above a whisper. "Yes, suddenly this is the greatest thought. To do this right here. We met here, we all shared so much happiness here. We were going to get married anyway, probably. You know that. Yes, let's do this. Get married right here. We'll go to the embassy tomorrow. Or the consulate. Surely, there's an American consulate in Pusan. There will be chaplains on the bases around. GIs marry all the time. Let's do this, then, Wilson. The chaplains can guide us for what to do to get married and when."

I took a deep breath, then nodded yes, took another breath, and nodded yes again while looking nervously back at Sandra.

"It's what I want," I said. "I was just hoping to be sane. It's so sudden."

"All right then," the Frenchman said joyously.

"That's wonderful," the Dutch girl swooned.

"We're going to get married," I said feeling the glow.

Sandra leaned over to kiss me tenderly on the lips.

"Yes, there are so many chaplains on the bases," I mused. "I'm sure the embassy knows people, too. Clergy, justices, whoever. And how to do all this.

Maybe there's even a Korean Las Vegas around."

"Good sport, mate," the Brit cheered while clapping each of us on the back.

"It was worthy of me to move out," Chaim said with a broad smile. "Ordained somehow."

"That very good, very good," the hostel owner cheered as he also patted us on the back. "I have brother. Good singer. He sing you song for your wedding. It called 'Love Rain.' That my wife and my love song. So, now for you too. Wonderful."

"Oh, yes, 'Love Rain,' " the Korean girls repeated.

"Tell your parents," I said to Sandra. "I'll call mine to let them know. I can't expect them to come so far on sudden notice. But yours can come easily."

"We're really going to do this," she said. "I love this!"

"I love you, Sandra," I said as I kissed each of her hands. "We have so much to work out. Where will we go to school? We're not that far from graduating. It's so abrupt. I don't want to split back up. We need to go to school together, but where?"

"We'll figure it out," she replied.

"I'm sure of that," I said.

Chapter 24

"All right," Matt Jillette yelled out through his bullhorn to everyone on the set. "The Yanks have turned the war in Korea around. We're wrapping up the movie now. MacArthur has produced, and morale is high once again. Right here where we're filming. This area, anyway. The allies were pinned down in Pusan. Nowhere else to go. Now they've got the Communist forces backing off. Or at least stymied. If you know history, the battle of Inchon is forthcoming.

"So we need to set the mood in this next scene. Some celebration for the new environment in this war going on. All the extras in combat gear, we need you to form up on the road nearby. The assistant directors will instruct you. You need to be in a winning mood. You can smell victory. And you need to sing. Don't worry, we will not give you sound, but sing anyway. We will edit in the real singing. Occasionally, we will have a close up of some of you singing. All the words you need to know are 'Hoorah, hoorah, we bring the jubilee.' I'll leave it to the assistant directors which soldiers marching will sing that line. Only that one line. As easy as it is, those assigned that line must practice it. Look authentic as you sing. So really sing. Then another group on cue will sing 'While we were marching through Georgia.'

I openly moaned. Loud enough that Matt Jillette

heard me as I was standing near the main actors in his vicinity.

"What is the problem over there?" the director asked with a bite. "Roy Holland, that man next to you. He's your double, isn't he? Is there a problem? We don't need him anymore if he has a problem with us."

I shook my head that I had no problem.

"Are you sure?" Jillette asked still showing frustration.

"I'm sorry, sir," I answered. "I'm from Texas, and this song is about General Sherman in the Civil War marching through Georgia."

"Yes," Jillette answered. "You know your history. You don't have to sing it if you don't want. Nor any other Johnny Reb in the crowd among us. Or you can compromise and be in the section of soldiers marching that will be singing the first line I gave you. About the jubilee. Let us know, and we'll accommodate anyone that has a problem with General Sherman."

Matt Jillette let out a laugh.

"Is that all right with you, Roy Holland's double?"

He looked me straight in the eye and let out another laugh.

"What's your name, young man?" he asked me.

"Wilson, sir."

"They call him Superman," Roy Holland remarked with a laugh of his own.

"Do they now? Superman, is it? I am not even going to ask where you got that tag. Maybe I should have used you more, if your name fits you."

I nodded and eased into a grin.

"All right," the director chided. "The Rebs can sing about the jubilee and the rest will sing about marching through Georgia. Are we set now?"

He gave a token pause then looked at one of the assistant directors with a nod to form us into marching groups.

"I didn't know you were still fighting the Civil War," Roy Holland joked.

"I'm not," I replied. "Just a habit, I guess. Culture. I'm a proud Texan, but I didn't realize how far I carried it."

"Don't worry about it," he said. "You got his attention. In a good way, even. It was colorful. Go find our jubilee group and enjoy yourself."

Chaim followed me as I walked toward the group designated as the jubilee group.

"I will be a Johnny Reb with you," he said with a smirk. "You make things fun."

"Good," I answered. "We need more Rebs."

It was an assistant director I never worked with before who was in charge of the jubilee group. He left us to ourselves in a loose mob form, until he was sure he had all he needed.

"So I hope you are going over your one line," the assistant director said. "The one to be sung. You will simply sing this one line over and over again until I inform you there is no more need. You will form in a loose formation now in front of me. What I mean by that is we don't need you in strict rows and columns, or all lined up in straight lines. This will be a forced march formation. I will call out a military cadence of *one two three four, one two three four*. Once we have the rhythm of the cadence down, I will have you sing your one line. This is the jubilee group. If you meant to be in the marching through Georgia group, you must go to it now. It should make no never mind to everyone but our Superman here."

He stared at me with a half-smile.

"But if you want to be in the marching through Georgia group, then now is the time."

He paused for a moment to see if anyone left the group. He then arranged us into our marching formation.

"We will have four men across per row, with one row immediately behind another, and march along this road in front of us. Listen to my cadence to get the rhythm and stay loosely in the formation you are now in. It is more a forced march than it is rigid, but we must stay in our rows of four, and no row should straggle. Remain loosely equidistant behind the row in front of you. After I give a cadence, I will then sing the one line you will need to sing. Sing it with me, my speed and rhythm. All this will be edited later. All that will show up is the company of you marching along the road and occasionally a close-up of some of you singing about the jubilee. Remember, you're one line to sing will simply be, 'Hoorah, hoorah, we bring the jubilee.' Only that. Sing it along with the others. If a few of you are not perfectly in step as you march or in sync with your singing, or miss a word, don't worry, it will be edited. But there should be no one mocking the cadence or the chorus along the way. You will be removed if you do not take this scene seriously. We won't waste time and film on horseplay. I hope that is clear."

He paused and stared at us again.

"It's simple," he continued. "Are there any questions?"

After a few seconds he looked at me.

"Are you okay with this, Superman?" he asked straight-faced, though I was sure he was in a kidding mood.

"I've got it down," I replied.

"Good," he said with a nod.

Even though forced marches were not as succinct and rigid as a company-type review, it required a few takes to get the scene believable. The road was long that we were on, so it did not require regrouping. We had only to improve the march or the up-close singing parts while continuing onward.

"Wilson," Roy Holland called out to me at the end of filming for the day. "I heard congratulations are in order for you."

I looked at him curiously, wondering what he was talking about. Except somehow I knew.

"I heard you're getting married," he continued as he held out his hand to celebrate. "Right here, with one of the girls. One of the extras. The one of them you insisted to be in scenes with you at times. That's wonderful. The Israeli guy told me. We were chatting about what happens next in our lives, after filming completes next week. That makes more sense now, why you pushed her to be with you when you could. I'm glad it all worked out for you. When does the wedding occur?"

"We're trying to arrange it all now," I replied.

"Well, let me know. The movie is wrapping up soon, and I'd like to celebrate with you, if it happens during the time I'm still here."

He seemed to mean it.

"Sure, thank you very much. I'll let you know.

Sandra's parents are getting involved now. Sandra is my fiancée. She's an extra from Texas, like me. We met and hit it off. Obviously. Her parents are at a base in Seoul and know people, chaplains and lawyers and such."

"Is it complicated?" he asked. "I suppose it could be, this being a foreign country to us and all. Well, keep me informed."

I was flattered a Hollywood star would care about my private life, since I was just one of the masses. It felt normal to me by now to be on the set as part of the environment, but I still knew my place. Any thought or courtesies thrown my way through the weeks were appreciated but had seemed to be token until now.

I absorbed this gesture by Roy Holland. As if I belonged. I enjoyed the feel of it.

Chapter 25

"Tomorrow is the last day on the set," the Aussie commented, back at the commons area after another day of filming. "I'm not sure if on the set is the correct wording, since we're always outdoors waiting to see where they're going to use us, if at all. It seems awkward now to think of not being in that movie. I've only been here a few weeks, but I feel in some routine, or like a cog or something on a wheel."

"I know," the Brit reinforced. "I've been here two months now. It's been fun. Especially coming home at night, like now. What is everybody going to do now that we have our lives back?"

"Well, go to our Texan friends' wedding, for one thing," the Dutch girl said with a smile. "We finish filming tomorrow, and then next day we go to the chaplain on the base for the shindig. Perfect ending."

"Yes, that's more exciting than making the movie," Chaim uttered cheerfully.

"For sure," Sunshine seconded. "Perfect timing. We won't miss the movie. A good memory, but it's the mates here that we'll miss. And the marriage of our comrades is the perfect ending. The movie ends, and our lovebirds here will ride off into the sunset with our blessing and support. I so wish this could be in the movie. I almost brought it up to Matt Jillette today. Maybe they could find a way to have a scene of two

American refugees or something, who fell in love during the war. They get married and end the film that way."

"Yes!" Chaim exclaimed. "That would be perfect. At least for us. Like our own little family reunion every time we see the movie through the years. Assuming it's the classic we hope, and they play it on television now and then."

"Wouldn't that be fab?" the Brit asked enthusiastically. "Yes, what memories for us! And for our kids, if we ever get to see reruns of it through the years."

"Do you think the movie is that good?" the Nepalese asked. "That it comes back on television occasionally? How jolly for us, if so."

"With all the big names in this movie," the Brit added, "plus Jillette as the director, you would think it would get played on the telly through the years. They've spent millions in the production, and huge salaries alone for all these biggie actors."

"But I heard that it didn't come out so well," the Aussie commented. "That the producer interfered too much, and that the script wasn't so well done. It was a big endeavor, and there were snags in the production. Too many changes along the way."

"They'll edit it," the Brit said. "We don't know what the final cut will look like. This stuff happens. You're just hearing gossip."

The Aussie nodded, then shrugged.

"So when are your parents coming, Sandra?" Sunshine asked. "You only just got hold of them. Can they get here in time?"

"They'll be here tomorrow," Sandra responded. "I

didn't want to tell them anything until I knew we could get it arranged. That it was going to be legal and all. I talked to them only about an hour ago, after Wilson and I left the chaplain's office on the base near here. We had to take a taxi to get there. We came in from filming later than expected, and I was afraid everything would be closed. I mean the chaplain's office and all we needed. But they were so precious. They waited for us."

"We got there before five," I interjected.

"But we didn't know if we would make it by five," Sandra added. "We were supposed to be finished filming mid-afternoon, like I said. So I thought we would be back here earlier, but there is always something unexpected in these movie scenes. I know that's normal, but I thought we would be here mid-afternoon. So, to be sure, Wilson and I took a taxi to the base. Then I called my parents from the chaplain's office. At his expense, God love him. This chaplain has been so nice to us. Anyway, my parents will be here tomorrow and staying at the base hotel, also arranged by the chaplain."

"They can't see the movie being filmed?" Sunshine asked. "It's the last day. Their one chance to see you on the set."

Sandra shook her head.

"I have no idea where we're going tomorrow," she responded. "I could have asked, but I don't have a clue where any place is, and even if I knew the name of the town nearby where the filming is going on, I still wouldn't know how to explain to them how to get there, since I don't know how to get anywhere. And we're all nobodies. Matt Jillette gets bugged when groupie types are around. I don't want to rock the boat.

It'll be okay. They'll see the movie and remember the wedding. So it's okay. You can't have everything."

"Yes, you can," the Aussie retorted.

"They would just see us standing around all day," I reinforced. "They would get on our case for wasting all this time doing this movie stuff when we came here for research."

"It will be great for them to see you two get married," the Frenchman came in. "You did the right thing. They will be happy to meet Superman, here, and see their daughter get married to another Texan."

"I met them already in Seoul," I interrupted. "Anyway, yes, we're just going to be standing around tomorrow, and I don't want to answer to anybody about neglecting our research for what they will call a bunch of nonsense."

"Your parents will not be flying in from Texas?" the Nepalese asked me.

"I only told them last night on the phone," I replied. "We were lucky to get this arranged at all. The chaplain was so helpful, or we would have to get married back in Texas. We needed to get married here to get it all legal. You know, about our status in school. Where we're going to go and such. Sandra still has a semester of classroom and has to be in Canyon, where West Texas State is located, and then she'll come live with me in College Station. That's sort of near Houston, where Texas A&M is located. They're excited, but they know we need to get this done so we can get back to Texas ASAP."

"What's ASAP?" the Frenchman asked.

"As soon as possible," Sunshine answered. "It stands for as soon as possible."

"So everything is settled, then," Chaim said. "This has been so much fun. I hate that we'll all be breaking up camp now, but this has been a blast. Good American word here. It's been a blast, my friends."

"That it has," the Aussie said cheerfully. "But now what? What's our encore? Not counting the marriage itself."

"What will you do, bloke?" the Brit asked him. "Go back to the colonies?"

"Bleedin' hell, mate," the Aussie said with a laugh. "You Brits are limey bastards, for certain. Oz is not a colony. The Brits think they still own us?"

"Yeah, well, are you going back to Oz, mate, or what?" the Brit inquired further.

"I want to go to Japan first," the Aussie replied. "It's so close. It would be a waste to not check the place out. I'll fly home from Tokyo. But first Hawaii. I've always wanted to see paradise."

"That's great," Sunshine said. "I might go with you, then. Japan, then Hawaii. Super. But our lovebirds here from Texas, as well as Chaim and I, will be in another movie first. Our director friend asked us again just yesterday if we intended to be in the movie he arranged for us with this other director we met. Let us see if we can arrange for any of you to also be extras. We didn't want to say anything to anyone because we didn't know when this movie would finish and if the offer would still be there for us about the other movie. Why don't all of you wait here another few days and let us see if there is room for you?"

"Yes, Sunshine and myself, with our Texas friends, will be in another movie," Chaim reinforced. "The director needs some Americans. Or European types, I mean. We would love to try to get everyone here to be with us. We've spoken with him about it. We didn't want to get anyone's hopes up."

"There's an update," I added. "Research will be the honeymoon for Sandra and me. So we aren't going to be in that other movie after all. Maybe that will help get some of y'all parts as extras in it."

"You mean that day the four of you went away with the assistant director alone to another area wasn't for our movie that we're just finishing up together now?" the Brit asked. "You didn't tell us."

"We felt guilty," I confessed. "This assistant director worked with us quite often and liked us and saw how we were in special parts a lot. He offered to help us with this other movie, and we checked it out. But Sandra and I need to get back to Texas, after some research here first. We'll be staying mostly with Sandra's parents while we do that. So please, give the movie a try."

"You would rather work on your college thesis than be Hollywood stars?" the Dutch girl asked mockingly.

"What kind of marriage will you two have, then?" the Frenchman moaned. "Two nerds. Heaven help you!"

"What kind of kids will they raise?" Sunshine joked.

"They will all sing 'Home On The Range' together, I am certain," Chaim added.

"Lord help them," the Brit came in. "But now every time I hear this bloody song, which will happen some my entire life, I will think of everyone here. So will Sandra and Superman as they raise their children and hear it. And sing it. I know also they will not treat it as some children's cowboy song, which will also give memories of our time here together. New meaning for an old song. This indeed will be a glorious wedding."

"Sounds good to me," I said. "Another reason we're getting married here. There couldn't be a better send-off to our marriage than this. And all of you."

Chapter 26

"Here he is," Lance Talbert greeted as some of the movie cast stared at Sandra and me when we arrived for our last day of filming. "We have heard, my dear fellow, that there are congratulations in order for you two."

Roy Holland wrapped his arm around my shoulders while Lance Talbert reached out to shake my hand. The other actors, behind him, smiled approvingly.

"I was told you were just an extra," Lance Talbert said as I remained frozen and speechless. "I don't mean that in a demeaning way. I took for granted you were an aspiring young actor, making his mark. Much like we all were at one stage of our journey in movies. Roy, here, has worked with you. I should have figured out you were simply his double, since indeed you were that. But you had parts and seemed to be everywhere with us, even if you didn't have parts directly with any of us but Roy. But it was explained to me just now that you and your young lady came here all the way from Texas just to be in this movie. That you are doing research for a thesis for a Master's degree. That is very impressive. Above and beyond, as they say."

"Where did you hear all of this?" I finally squeaked out. "It's true, but why would anyone bother telling you any of this?"

"I mentioned it this morning while we were

preparing makeup," Roy Holland commented. "How you two met here on the set, fell for each other, and are getting married tomorrow. It was a charming story, and I thought the others might enjoy it. A human-interest type story, you know."

"But who bothered to tell you this?" I asked, showing my amazement.

"The Israeli that works sometimes in stunts," Roy Holland related further. "Chaim is his name. You know him. You worked together. I was taken by both of you through the weeks. You both were always reliable and competent. Today being the last day, I thought I would chat with Chaim about what he was going to do next. I liked he was Israeli and wanted to get to know him a bit more. Then, in the conversation, you two getting married came up. I had asked about you somewhere in all the chat, you know. So congratulations are in order. I thought I would mention a charming story like this to the others. A nice ending to our movie here. A nice twist, I mean."

"Let's talk to Matt," one of the actresses suggested. "Let's get a scene of these two lovelies somehow. Fit it in somewhere in the movie. A charm for the likes of us, even if no one else gets it when they watch the movie."

"Oh, no," I said trying not to gulp. "Please, he can't be bothered with this. It's the last day. He'll not want to mess around with this."

"He's pretty pragmatic, for sure," one of the actors said with a chuckle. "But it's worth a try. Last day and all. He might get a kick out of it. Lighten things up a bit. You *are* getting married tomorrow. That may set a mood in him."

I made ready to say more, but struggled to regain

my composure.

"There Matt is," one of the actors said. "I'll go talk to him."

"He's going to hate my guts," I said with a whimper.

"For getting married?" an actress asked while giving a wink. "Even Matt can be charmed, I think."

I watched the actor on my behalf begin to talk to Matt Jillette. Occasionally he looked our way and once even pointed toward me. Matt Jillette seemed unphased. Finally, the conversation ended, and the director looked quickly at his watch.

I nervously watched the actor who had made the sales pitch about me walk back our way.

"He wouldn't go for it," the actor explained. "He wants to wrap things up. We all have to fly to Rome in a few days to do scenes in meeting rooms and hotels. Bungalows and such, you know. Indoor scenes. But I kept insisting how this would be a human-interest angle and make for a good publicity story. He wouldn't buy any of it, but I got it through to him that this is exactly the kind of thing that comes up somewhere in a gossip column. Makes things seem down to earth. Things people can relate to. I promised it would be a short scene, a few seconds long. That we would do it where the lighting and cameras were already in sync."

The actor looked at me grinning. Somehow, something was going to come of this.

"They call you Superman, don't they?" the actor asked. "That helped sell things. He remembers this Superman guy. He seems to be game now. He's seen you around and knows your nickname. We all thought you were a bit actor. More than just a walk-on extra, you know. And he remembered you favorably for trying to talk him out of singing General Sherman's taunt, you know, back when the troops had to sing about marching through Georgia. You irritated him and he thought you obnoxious, but he actually got a kick out of it. So, Superman, I think we're in. You and your fiancée here are going to run toward each other, hug, then kiss. All in about five seconds of filming. Somewhere it will fit perfectly, warm up an otherwise gory scene."

"I will see to it myself," Lance Talbert said chirpily. "He had to pay me two million dollars to get me in this movie and put up with making this debacle. I'll remind him how my happiness is important to him. He'll think me bluffing, but it will help seal the deal. What do you say, Superman?"

My heart was fluttering, and I could feel my throat tighten. How on God's earth did something like this happen to me? With Sandra here to witness. A quick close-up of us as we hugged and kissed suddenly arranged. A perfect golden anniversary viewing—if we lived that long—to celebrate.

I broke away from Sandra to tell Chaim and Sunshine, who were nearby.

"Don't you make something like this up," Sunshine chastised as she studied me, trying to believe my story.

"He's telling the truth," Sandra reinforced. "Please, find all our companions from the hostel that are here. It will take away if they miss this."

"They aren't far," Chaim said. "They always hang out together, and never far from us, since sometimes we get special treatment in a scene because of you. They want to be ready just in case some of the good luck spills over to them. I'll find them. Go back to the set."

I was nervous, even more so than when I had to audition as a stuntman. I could see myself tripping as I ran to Sandra in our new scene together. Or slamming into her. Or not kissing her on the lips but slurping instead.

"Don't overact," I reminded myself once again. I then looked nervously at Sandra.

"Just wait on me," I coached her. "It's okay if you look nervous, so don't worry about it. We're in love in the scene and excited to see each other. So nervous can fit. Somehow, we are being reunited and the war is over, I suppose, and here we are finding each other again. Just wait on me. I'll try not to throw up all over you."

"Oh, shush," she said with a giggle.

Her calmness relaxed me. I could feel it. I could do this. Someday Sandra and I were going to get a copy of this movie for ourselves and our posterity and play it on our anniversary for the rest of our lives.

Chapter 27

"Well, hello," I greeted our neighbor as I opened the front door. "Come on in."

"Good afternoon, Wilson. I wanted to return the DVD you lent. The movie you were in. But I never saw you or Sandra in it. I'm not being skeptical, but are you sure you're not teasing?"

"It was toward the end," I answered. "Right at the end, in fact. I was the guy that ran to the girl at the side of the road, and we hugged, then kissed. It was only a couple of seconds. I had a trimmed beard they pasted on me, and Sandra wore a wig with long flowing hair. The actors who helped set up the scene thought we would be noticed better, stand out from the crowd. But it only confused you. Great!"

"I don't remember any bearded guy at the end hugging a girl on the road."

"It was a quick little scene," I said as I shook my head in frustration. "But there was a close-up of us. We were on the edge of the crowd there."

My friend stared back at me blankly.

"Doesn't matter," I moaned. "That's why I never bring it up. I'd have to lend out my DVD and then explain a short, insignificant scene. Don't know why I brought it up now, except that I saw the documentary about making the movie on YouTube. We were in that documentary. I guess because of Lance Talbert, but I really don't know. He was so gracious to us. It has a still picture of the main actors in it, and we were in the picture with them, too. We were at the side of the group of cast members, even though we were nobodies. The actors in it insisted, since we were getting married and I had been in a lot of scenes before. It's a great memory for us, but I guess nobody else."

"If you say so, Wilson. I enjoyed the movie. It was okay, anyway. I like Lance Talbert as much as the next guy, though. Big fan of his. But I don't care much for MacArthur. Not because of Lance Talbert's acting, though. Anyway, thanks for lending me your DVD."

He handed it to me and abruptly turned to leave.

"It's great not having to bother with humility," I said to Sandra with a chuckle as I closed the door behind him.

"Our own kids didn't believe us at first," she said indifferently. "Even after seeing us in the closeup scene at the end. It didn't show us that well, I know. But well enough. I mean, they grew up with us when we still looked like we did back then. They gave us the benefit of the doubt. Or pretended to, anyway. Our own children don't fully believe us. How does that work?"

"All good memories," I commented. "The documentary was made later on. The kids, at least, recognized us in the photo in it. So they have to believe us that we really were in that movie. I can't believe we didn't get a copy of the photo."

"Oh, Wilson, you know why we don't have a copy of the photo. The picture was taken the very last afternoon we were there. After all the Korean scenes were complete. Just before all the big shots went to Rome for studio scenes. We were nobodies. Me more so than you. You at least got on the inside with them, sort of. No one was going to bother to get us a photo."

"They didn't even give us credits at the end," I whined further.

Sandra reached up and hugged my neck.

"You know the answer to that too," she said with a laugh. "They didn't know our names."

"Roy Holland knew who I was. And Matt Jillette."

"I'm sure Matt Jillette forgot your name five minutes after he acknowledged you that time. Roy was probably long gone by the final editing and didn't have a say in putting you on the credits or not. You just got your little feelings hurt and are still whining."

"Somebody's got to do the whining," I joked.

"But the movie made for a great romance between us and can count as a honeymoon too, even though we didn't get married until the day after we finished filming. So who needs a credit or an Oscar? I won a Wilson. That's even better."

"We went to the cinema there in College Station when the movie came out and barely recognized ourselves," I pouted further.

"And we turned down the chance to make another movie after the one about Pusan," she returned. "We knew what we wanted, and it was academics and each other. I have no regrets. I doubt we would have ever made a dent in Hollywood, but we made a small ripple at least once, with this movie, and we let it tease us through the years. For the millionth time, so there."

"I don't whine that much," I said. "I don't even think about it that much. I didn't enjoy the Hollywood part of it except for the novelty and supposed glamour. And with all the egos, I wanted as far away from

Hollywood as I could possibly get. But still, it does come to haunt when the subject comes up. Like when a rerun of it comes on TV. Or we slip and mention something to a neighbor, who thinks we're lying."

˙ "I loved our friends at the hostel that were in the movie with us," Sandra said nostalgically. "Those are the real memories to me. That and meeting you and getting married. It's fun to think about the movie, but it was the times and the friends at the hostel that matter to me."

"Speaking of which, I wish we could have a reunion. But we never saw any of them again. They were excited to make another movie, and we were excited to get back to research and school and start our domestic life. I got Sunshine's address, and Chaim got mine. Then we lost contact anyway. I do wish we could meet again."

"We meet our friends again every time that movie appears somewhere," she answered. "And this way we don't have to worry if one of them was killed in a car wreck later on or if someone became an alcoholic. We have wonderful memories of everyone and visions of what they probably became in their lives. We met Lance Talbert and watched every old spy movie Matt Jillette directed, and then moved on. How many people have these kinds of memories?"

"And even better," I said with a grin, "I know our friends from there teach their kids 'Home On The Range.' Our vagabond companions at the hostel, I mean. They raised their kids right because of us. Wherever they are, our old friends at the hostel look at the heavens and think of us because of that song."

"Life is so precious, Wilson. It's like your

committee chairman said when I met him that first time when we got home. Life is the great university, and then we graduate. I love thinking how we'll all meet again in that great grad school in the sky."

"Used to be cowboy imagery about all that for us. Heaven and all. Now we have St. Peter handing out diplomas to get in."

"With God directing," she added. "That part never changes."

A word about the author...

Born in Harlingen, Texas on October 7, 1948, I grew up and worked on a cotton farm, graduated from Harlingen High School in 1966, and attended Texas A&M beginning in the summer of 1966.

In January 1970 I dropped out to enlist in the United States Marine Corps, where I served as an enlisted man attaining the rank of sergeant, with an honorable discharge after three years.

I worked as a computer programmer afterward in Houston and as a civil servant for a US Air Force Base in Frankfurt, Germany. I traveled and worked in Europe for two years, which included flying to Israel in October 1973 to aid the Jewish State in the Yom Kippor War. I was also in Greece in the summer of 1974 when war between Greece and Turkey erupted over Cyprus. I was stuck on the Greek island of Ios for part of that war, until I managed to catch a boat to Athens just in time to watch the Greek military dictatorship fold.

I returned to Texas A&M in the fall of 1976 to finish my Bachelor's degree in Business Management, and returned to Europe afterward and also Israel where I lived for almost a year. Later I taught English in Taiwan before returning home to get a Master's degree in Agricultural Economics in 1980, which I received in 1982.

I joined the US Peace Corps in 1984 and served for three years in the Philippines. In 1987, I began work for the Swiss government as a computer programmer until 1998. I have worked in the IT department of Texas A&M since 1998. I have three children and am presently divorced. I am Jewish.

www.ingramcontent.com/pod-product-compliance
Lightning Source LLC
Chambersburg PA
CBHW060939180626
46817CB00004B/1623